AUTUMN'S RITE

BY A.R WOLFE

To my Fiancé

Who told me to write a book about ghost sex;

so I wrote this instead.

xx

CHAPTER ONE

Sunlight streamed its way into her consciousness. Kallie opened her eyes briefly before tossing around, looking for her cell phone.

Damn!

She had forgotten to set her alarm and now it was 8a.m—she was late for work. She craved her routine morning jog to clear the cobwebs from her mind, but time was a luxury she couldn't afford today.

She dashed into the shower for a quick wash, running a comb through her wet hair. She picked up a crisp white silk shirt to go with her favourite grey pencil skirt that stopped just above her knees. She eyed herself in the bathroom mirror and quickly applied some mascara to her tired green eyes. The same eyes her mother had. The thought of her caused a sharp tug on her stomach but she pushed it aside, focusing on her appearance again. She tried to tame her wavy, ashy blonde hair into a ponytail and gave up with an exasperated sigh, leaving it to cascade down her back.

A light touch of powder over her freckles and gloss on her lips—that'll have to do.

Keys, where the hell did I put the keys?!

She checked if Hana, her roommate and best friend, had come back from her night shift working at the bar downtown, she walked into the kitchen and by the messy sight that welcomed her it was pretty obvious: Hana was definitely home. Red plastic cups scattered the kitchen bench; Kallie lifted one of the offending cups to her nose and sniffed—was that whisky? Hana was an amazing friend but she could learn a thing or two about tidiness. Kallie poured the brown substance down the sink before tossing the cup into the open trash can. She relayed memories of her and Hana talking time and time again about cleaning up, but Hana was less of a 'clean-up-as-you-go' person, and more of a 'clean-up-when-you've-lost-something-and-can't-see-the-floor' kind of person. Kallie cleared the thought from her mind as she continued searching for her car keys under all the junk.

After what seemed like forever she found them under a half-eaten double cheese and pepperoni pizza, Hana's favourite. Kallie shook her head, hurriedly locked the door to their modest two bedroom cottage, and stepped out to leaves swirling around her, a slight chill in the air.

Morning, Baby.

She ran her slender fingers over the sleek roof top of her black Chevrolet Camaro, this was an unspoken ritual, and it was her way of starting her ride each day. Her ride was old but lovingly restored—one of the few luxuries she allowed herself.

She drove fast, missing her leisurely cruise through her favourite city sights. The locality was an eclectic mix of nationalities, thanks to the large university that occupied it. It was also where Kallie worked. She loved the energy and free-spirited nature of its residents; it was a blend of various exciting energies and mostly delightfully watching students go about their activities. That summer had been particularly hot and the mild autumn was a welcome change for everyone. The trees were starting to turn those beautiful shades of brown and orange with that crispness in the air—the kind that made you feel like change was coming. She pulled onto North Pleasant Street, passing her favourite bakery and coffee shop. No time for a bagel today.

Amherst has always been a remarkable place with its hiking paths, trails and groves of pines and maples, the trees seem to sing in the wind with their rich history of the town.

Kallie had grown up here. She attended the local middle school where she met Hana. She loved this town and all its cultural values. Icons like Emily Dickinson, Robert Frost, and others had made their home here, and she had as well.

After Kallie had graduated college in New York finishing her Masters in Folklore and Mythology, she moved back, bringing with it all the bitter-sweet memories of her father and his death five years prior. She never thought she'd return but the memories of home called to her, the last piece of her dad that she had left, including the cottage he had left her in his will.

Charles Rosen was a man of few words. He was tight-lipped about Kallie's mother, save only some vague remarks about her kindness and some unfortunate situation that drew her away from them. He would sit in his favourite chair and lapse into a daydream whenever the topic of her mom came up; it made her dejected to watch the sadness that would tinge his face. She had so many questions but she could not get any answers to them. She became tired of having those questions, tired of putting her father in a place where he constantly had to revisit his past pain. So she decided to give it time, but time with her father was snatched away.

Growing up, as Kallie's father grew distant, she turned to her Grandmother. She enjoyed listening to her mystical stories of princesses, of witches, of werewolves and goblins. She would then imagine her mother to be a beautiful queen and weave elaborate stories about where she was and where she had been all these years. Off saving kingdoms and their people. She needed answers, even if they were fictional. There was of course a mystery surrounding where her mother was and growing up she had been fascinated by the world her grandmother had painted in her stories.

Her grandmother, Mary, was a lovely person with just the right amount of sweet and tartness that made Kallie adore her all the more. Mary was an intelligent woman and could see that Kallie was a smart, sensitive child with a vivid imagination and curious nature. She was the one responsible for Kallie growing up with lots of love and attention in the Rosen household.

Her father worked as a curator in one of the museums in town before his accident. He was tall and waif-like, much like Kallie, but with warm brown eyes that always looked at things from afar, quietly. He used to take her to the local coffee shop, the one with his favourite flavour of ice-cream. They'd go there after school if her grades had been good. Hell, they went even if they were bad. He always got the same: mint chocolate chip, two scoops, in a waffle cone. *Bleurgh.* She always hated that flavour. Now she couldn't stand it.

Kallie shook her head, as if she could shake the memories from her mind and turned her car down the elm-lined pathway leading to the University of Massachusetts. She hated getting distracted before work, especially with exams and paper grading coming up fast. Kallie pulled up, put it in park and exhaled loudly tapping the steering wheel. She needed to focus today and thinking about Dad, Mom, and the past isn't helping.

She loved her job; being an ancient mythology and folklore professor is her passion but sometimes paper grading gets a bit tedious. She sighed again.

I need coffee and lots of it.

Kallie ran lightly up the stairs to the cafeteria.

Thank God, the line is small but that also means I'm late, she thought exasperatedly as she slid to the back of the line praying for it to move quickly. Her turn came and she placed her order, "Two double shot espressos with cream and a chicken sandwich".

She stuffed the sandwich into her bag and started walking towards her office balancing the coffees in her arms. Walking quickly while drinking a super-hot coffee was no mean task, and Kallie was glad that she didn't slop it on herself.

One small espresso down, she reached her office, and took a quick look. Her department Head, Dr Richard Gale, was not at his desk, which was good. Maybe he won't notice her tardiness. Her only other colleague in the mythology department, Shirley, was absorbed in her papers, but waved a friendly greeting towards Kallie. She waved back, slid into her office, picked up a bunch of term papers and started her work at her desk.

She was fairly new to this college, but she loved the people and atmosphere it exuded. She'd never been inside the university before starting her position, and her first visit for the interview process made her fall in love; the old chapel on the college grounds was a favourite, the architecture a stunning backdrop against the fall leaves. She remembered how anxious she had been, as it was her first job interview after graduating, but Dr Gale, in spite of his fame and importance, was a very down-to-earth guy. His kind blue eyes and smile made her feel comfortable instantly.

Thinking about her boss brought her focus back to her papers, she had to finish these, and she was frustrated.

Why am I thinking about all this crap today?

Kallie's mind was buzzing, probably also from the espresso she just chugged, and she'd also been sleep deprived for the past few weeks. Working on her PhD thesis regarding the presence and rituals of Mythical Creatures from Vampires, Faeries and Elves, awake at all hours will do that to a woman. She was on a mission, crunching book after book, interviewing senior and amateur historians and anyone else she could find in connection with them. Her work consumed her, but she absolutely loved it. She didn't mind losing her sleep for her work, although her Friday night club-hopping with Hana definitely wasn't helping, but someone had to keep an eye on her and her hijinks. She was in the last phase of her research and could feel it stirring something inside her, like something in her had been asleep for 26 years and it was finally waking up. She was restless, but she couldn't put her finger on it—like she was staring at a big wall of darkness and she had to push through it soon, into the unknown. She closed her eyes and rested her head on the window ledge near her chair.

"Feeling the winds of change?"

Dr. Gale was standing right in front of her. Kallie jumped up and smiled sheepishly at her boss.

"Sorry, Richard" she said quickly. "I haven't been sleeping enough lately."

Almost like he already expected her response he smiled with a twinkle in his eyes.

"You're working yourself to the bone. Soon you'll be joining your own vampire coven with those hooded eyes and late nights." he laughed jokingly. "I came here to remind you about the meeting with the College Head regarding your funding for the project; it has been postponed to this afternoon".

Kallie gathered her thoughts again.

"Oh yes, of course. Thank you for reminding me."

"It's been set for 1:30pm, after the lunch break, OK? I'll see you then." He walked off towards his office. Kallie had indeed forgotten, but more funding for her project also meant more resources for research. Much needed research. Maybe she could finally visit Salem. Kallie smiled as new-found energy bubbled inside of her, she flipped open her laptop finally feeling ready to take on the day.

CHAPTER TWO

She was halfway through her papers when she had a strange feeling of being watched, tingles on the back of her neck making her hair stand on end. She turned and stood up fast, startled.

A tall, dark haired man was sitting on the edge of her desk, watching her with a slight sardonic smile. She couldn't tear her eyes off of him; he was beyond handsome, striking even. He stood up gracefully, his amber eyes were piercing, his cheek-bones stood out with perfection, gradually sloping to the most perfect mouth she had ever seen. His hair shone a deep chocolate, and his skin was light with a slight 5 o'clock shadow.

"Do you always stare at your visitors with such intensity?" He smirked.

Kallie shut her mouth quickly she had a terrible habit of staring with her mouth wide open, and blushed furiously.

Who is this guy? He threw her completely off guard, turning her into a bumbling school girl.

"I'm sorry, I wasn't aware I had a meeting with… with you, with anyone".

She was aware of the limpid counter and chided herself. Where were her smarts when she really needed them? Her cool, calm demeanour had suddenly escaped her. He raised one of his eyebrows and his lips lilted up ever so slightly at one corner.

"How surprising. Your assistant didn't tell you I was stopping by? I had specifically requested for you, although you are not at all what I expected." As he said this, he threw a speculative look at her, eyeing her up and down. Kallie realised she was staring again and mentally shook herself.

A lopsided smirk escaped his lips as he locked eyes with her again making Kallie's insides do a dance. "What, exactly, were you expecting?"

Now he was the one staring. Why?

"I'm sure my capabilities will not astonish you once your mind wraps around the fact that brains and beauty are not disjointed."

Kallie's turn to smirk, "Now, is there something I can help you with?" she chided him, taking a seat once more, smoothing her skirt with her hands. He looked surprised as if that was the exact thought running through his mind.

He paused for what seemed like a full minute, sat down, and replied, "I didn't mean to demean you. I was only perplexed at your age. Professors of your calibre are rarely so young." Kallie blinked, unsure of how to take the backhanded compliment.

The man leaned in continuing, "I was told that you are researching the age-old rituals of mythological creatures and I am curious whether you came across any information regarding vampires and their specific ceremonies during your research?" His voice grew mellow and sounded dreamy to her, as though putting her into a trance. She shook her head absentmindedly to get rid of the foggy feeling clouding her mind, like a large fluffy blanket was hugging her tightly.

He looked intensely at her, frustration registering mildly on his face. She had no idea why, but she felt he was somehow disappointed.

"Who told you this?" Kallie queried the man, who still had a frustrated look daubed on his face.

"Look, even if I had come across any information, why should I share them with you? You haven't told me anything about yourself, or your credentials…I have no idea who you are. Are you a student here?" she said.

He stared firmly at her, but again confusion seeped through the cracks and his brow furrowed.

"What are you doing?" She asked, vexed.

"What?" He countered, with apparently feigned ignorance; she shifted uneasily under his stare.

He stood up and was next to her in a blink, she didn't know why, but she felt the need to stand up too, but unlike him, she was unable to move an inch. Her eyes were irresistibly locked into his, her hands gripping her chair. He whispered the words quickly in a chant, *"Quod nulla oblivione delebitur"*.

Kallie squinted, "What are you saying? Is that… is that Latin…?"

He was so close now that his dark, midnight stubble was almost touching her cheek—it set her heart alight, his woodsy smell making the blood course through her veins, her bloom in all the right places. She felt it thumping in her chest; surely he could see it through her blouse.

Calm down Kallie, you don't even know this guy. He could be a psychopath!

* * *

Theo was taken aback. Everything about her was an enigma to him.

Why wasn't it working? A human who seemed invulnerable to vampire charms.

He was surprised when he'd first seen her driving her car through the boulevard, then suddenly everything slowed around him. He had watched, stunned as her face, serene, yet thoughtful, broke into a smile at the trees.

Her halo was a beautiful, bright burnt orange-gold; a kind that he had never seen, he was perplexed. He longed to see her up close, to touch her blonde hair.

He whispered to himself considering how unusual her halo was, her aura threw him deep into his own thoughts.

Who is she…? He was wary of a growing uneasiness in him.

He should've turned back but his legs made their way to the building of their own accord. His senses had returned briefly and he decided to scout the place first before entering. It was a wise decision once he realised she was the professor he was indeed seeking.

The building that housed the History department was ancient; he could sense an undercurrent of unknown magic, maybe even primeval. It may of course be due to the rare artefacts housed throughout the department.

He needed to get in and get out quickly. He would be a blur, an electronic anomaly in the security cameras; hence, it would be best if he was seen by as few people as possible. He had already spied the wing housing the History and Mythology department. He then concealed himself. It was simple really. He camouflaged easily, he would go unnoticed. Anyone who looked at him would have seen a non-descript persona, an uninteresting being just carrying files or coffee. If asked to, a witness wouldn't be able to describe him, becoming confused. He quickly noted the placard: "Professor Kallie Rose". He eyed her from the doorway as she worked, her finger absentmindedly twirling her hair as she read from her papers.

He once again reviewed his plan. He would materialise in front of her, get whatever information she had on his mission, make her forget he was ever there and then disappear. And yet… He had a brief moment of worry. The fact that this human called to him so strongly could not be a good sign.

No sense turning back. I'll be in and out before anyone notices.

The professor dropped her head to her desk and he chuckled, she really was something. A much older man entered into her office, whose halo was the strangest shade of swamp green, and he discussed something with her briefly before leaving again.

A strange sense of exhilaration replaced his uneasiness as he plunged into the room…

And now, he couldn't make her *forget*.

She was still staring at him, her eyes darting back and forth, as though taking him all in, his mind raced in panic. His eyes were wide.

Shit. As though sensing his dilemma, Kallie's gaze softened; "Look, I don't know who you are, but if you want some information regarding the myths I am studying, I guess I can answer some questions for you. Please, sit." She gave a small smile.

Maybe she thinks I'm one of those fantasy creature fanatics, he thought. God knows there are enough of them, going insane searching for a sliver of real magic.

He was safe for now, but he must get away soon in case she decided to call security.

He smiled back at her and then sat in the chair opposite Kallie, calming himself.

* * *

"Professor, I am Theodore Westfall. I am very interested in your research in sub- and super-human transformations; I would appreciate if you would share any knowledge of their transformative rituals with me."

Kallie's interest in the strange man grew further. "That's an unusual question. I think I've seen a few ancient texts that mention them. I only have hear-say data regarding that, but I do hope that one of my sources will come through soon."

He looked immensely disappointed. Suddenly, as before, he had started to focus on her eyes and murmur under his breath. Kallie felt an irresistible force pulling her towards him, even as she breathed out. What felt like a lifetime later she snapped out of the reverie, irritated, "What are you doing?"

Now, it was his turn to look astonished, even a bit frightened. He blurted out, "Y-you are not… What are you…?"

With wide eyes, he turned swiftly and was off.

Kallie felt like she was turned to stone, she had seen her fair share of weirdos during her research—people claiming to be witches, vampires, the "real deal" they would say. Those people wouldn't know magic if it had hit them straight in the face. But then, there are a rare few who felt like "The Real Thing". Well, at least they did to Kallie. They were usually very careful when disclosing details though, and disappeared at any whiff of suspicion.

But, this… this was something beyond anything she'd ever come across, her mind played the entire experience over again—his super-human speed, his hypnotic looks and voice, his unimaginable good looks, but beyond all that, his sharp mind and quick wit. All that indicated that he was no fanatic trying to find mythical creatures, she couldn't make him out—already she had a strong yearning to know more about Theodore Westfall.

She flipped open her laptop again, determined to continue her day normally.

Kallie felt restless, she couldn't gather any coherent thoughts together let alone focus on work, but she needed to push it aside until she could really delve into the mystery while safe at home. She checked the time and realised it was nearly one thirty; she was going to be late to her funding meeting. Shit, shit! Grabbing her bag she raced out of her office and down the corridor.

The meeting ran late, but went surprisingly well. She gave a convincing argument even with her mind in its jumbled state. She grabbed her keys decided three thirty was a decent time to head home for the day. She needed to hash the events of today out to someone sane as she was feeling just a little bit crazy.

When she arrived home, Hana was conveniently absent.

Ugh dammit, Hana. She felt irritated. *Where was your best friend when you really needed her?*

At least the apartment was clean. Her irritation dulled slightly.

She slowly went through the events of the day, his last question hit home. What had he said? *"What are you?"* Well, with all the work she had been doing, she did feel like a zombie, but she shrewdly suspected that wasn't quite what he meant. She was puzzled.

She sighed and reluctantly admitted to herself that it had been a while since she had been so close to a man, and this Theo or whoever, was a man through and through. Kallie tried to stay awake for Hana, but her clock blinked red angry numbers at her and her eyes were heavy. 1:20AM. She groaned and crawled under her bed covers.

She slipped into a fitful sleep; her mind was trying to weave its way through the jumble of her thoughts. Once again her office came to view—he was there, but this time, she was unable to open her mouth or move, her eyes were locked into his, which glowed amber with desire, his mouth twisting into a cruel smile, as he made his way across the room. She was afraid.

He walked towards her, shirtless. Her fear was replaced with desire as his hands stretched out to grasp her face gently in his hands, his amber eyes slightly hooded and burning bright, he smelled fantastic: a blend of earth and musk mixed with something citrusy—she was swooning, her legs weakened and her breathing hitched. He held her for what felt like an eternity, their lips so close but never touching until finally, he touched his lips against hers, soft at first, then urgent.

His hands slid into her hair, tugging. He went deeper into her mouth as his hands trailed away to her silk shirt feeling her bust heave, kissing her with just as much hunger as she had burning inside of her. She locked her arms around his neck, feeling his hard torso against hers. He thrust her up, her legs around his waist, pushing her onto her desk, his hands on her breasts again; he flicked open one button, then another, his amber eyes teasing her before tearing the rest sending her blouse flying. She felt his firm abs, trailing circles around his clavicle, and felt him groan. Theo reached down; keeping one hand firmly around her back pressing against him, the other tugged her lace panties to one side as he slid her forward to the edge of the desk her skirt riding up. He traced her crevice, teasing her as she squirmed and longed for him. He leaned in closer, his stubble caressing her neck, whispering in her ear, "I want you to beg." He traced her some more before his fingers flicked her swollen nub and Kallie's breath caught in her throat; she moaned involuntarily arching her back, "Yes. God, please yes." She could feel herself soaking the desk beneath her before Theo's hand was replaced by his large shaft, throbbing hard, pressing against her entrance. He thrust slowly, then roughly, and she closed around him like two puzzle pieces fitting together perfectly. She cried out in pleasure as he rocked her against the desk. Kallie locked eyes with Theo once more, the amber in them changing to a fiery red, his mouth parted in pleasure.

She grabbed his hair, tugging as she climaxed, moaning louder than she'd ever had. He moaned, rearing up like a wild animal, lifting her from her desk and thrusting her against the wall, one arm pinned above her, her legs spread before locking around his waist, his hot mouth now roaming all over her: her neck, her arms. Her breasts were heaving, her body began to shake as she realised she was going to cum for a second time. He joined the primeval rhythm, trembling and churning. He locked eyes with her, grabbing her smooth neck with his spare hand. "Harder", she whispered, his grasp tightened as he choked her harder and quickened his pace, groaning. Kallie's eyes fluttered shut as pleasure overwhelmed her; she was floating somewhere, as her whole body lay throbbing, throbbing with pure pleasure and ecstasy. He laid his head against her neck, moaning in ecstasy, his lips grazed her ear, his voice gravelly:

"Pretty good… for a human."

Kallie woke with a start, breathing heavy. She was embarrassed to note that she was having a wet dream, let alone with a stranger she had met only briefly. If Theo could give her such wet dreams, she shuddered with pleasure to think about how he would be in reality.

CHAPTER THREE

Kallie woke up late the next morning after finally getting to sleep, but the difference between the day before and the present day could not have felt greater. She kept smiling to herself as she sped through her morning chores, not caring to give a glance at the clothes and papers lying on the floor. She raced to work, her thoughts straying back to Theo along the way; it was as though the dreams had awakened another side of her. She was not wholly opposed to this dreamy new version of herself. Dream Kallie was flirty and dangerous, having sex against walls. Her insides clenched as she remembered Theo's hands on her, his mouth against hers. She knew it was stupid, getting so worked up over a dream but she couldn't help it. Kallie pushed it to the back of her mind.

Her research was only halfway through, and she still needed to gather a few sources to get some details, but on the whole, she had enough information to start working on her thesis. Dr. Gale had promised to send her the details on the sources as soon as possible; thankfully, he was away on a conference today though. She felt that she couldn't bear to talk any more about her research.

As she tried to get her work done, flashes of her dream kept running through her mind, creating images and thoughts that made her mind go crazy, making her stomach clench fervidly. Was she under some sort of spell? No man had ever affected her this way. She leaned back against her chair with a huff, thinking about his lean, taut physique, his pale skin and his almost glowing, amber eyes.

Pretty good… for a human.

Kallie's eyes flicked open. What the hell, how had she only just remembered this? His voice replayed in her head three, four, five times over. *For a human.* **For. A. Human.** What? Clearly her work was spilling into her dream life.

Suddenly, a thought struck her. What if he wasn't human? Ha! She laughed out loud catching herself in her crazy thought process. I mean, she had come across stories of vampires, werewolves, and demonic beings in her work before and she had always believed a small part of them might stem from fact. But only a small portion. The reality of having physical contact with one of the creatures she imagined was not one she was ready for. She felt her legs tremble at the thought of it, it started to make sense: the effect he had on her, the control he imagined he had over her mind when he was at her office. Yet, he didn't have control—not full control anyway. She had questions.

If it were true, why would any magical being show itself to me? The dangers must be huge. And, if so, why would he need to come to me for my knowledge?

Kallie frowned, mystified. She knew from her research that mythical creatures lived in close-knit groups, always suspicious of everyone, even their own kind. *What can I possibly know that he doesn't already know from one of his own? Maybe he's been shunned or cast out from his kind?*

His speed and agility came to her mind— and then those eyes. The dream burst into her mind again causing Kallie to take a sharp breath. She couldn't have been more confused.

* * *

Dr. Shirley was working diligently on grading papers in the workroom, and Kallie felt guilty about skipping her own work. But her mind was too much for her to handle at the moment; the possibilities of Theo being anything supernatural had her mind running wild. She told Dr. Shirley she was not feeling well and was heading home for some rest.

Dr. Patcher looked at her, concerned. "You're working yourself too hard. Don't forget to take care of yourself. You can hand in the papers late, and don't worry; I will inform Dr. Gale for you". Kallie thanked Shirley and made her way to her car.

The day was a beautiful one—lazy, fall wind was up. On a whim, Kallie stopped her car and went out for a walk in the park. She had worn a long light-green chiffon skirt with a light cream shirt that day. The wind whipped her skirt playfully as she strolled passed dual-toned trees.

Kallie bought herself a coffee from the coffee cart and sat down on a bench, watching all the people; children, mothers, grandparents, babysitters, dog-walkers; there were so many. People-watching was a favourite past-time. She felt calm, serene even, for the first time in a very long time. The trees were beautiful shades of burnt orange and red, they always made her feel safe, at peace, like a haven. The sun was shining. The whole atmosphere had an unearthly mellow feel to it.

The next few moments were all bliss until she started having the now familiar feeling like she was being watched. It was only a matter of time before the thought crossed her mind; she turned around slowly.

He was standing next to the bench; she caught her breath and nearly choked on her coffee. "Oh, hi…" she said, wiping her mouth quickly. She wildly put a lid on her thoughts about her dream, trying to look normal as she blushed profusely, tucking a stray hair behind her ear. He kept looking at her with an inscrutable expression; it was laden with a kind of caution or even fear, his head tilted slightly. She couldn't understand it at all.

"I must speak with you. Please, I assure you that you will not come to any harm through me. But, before that, please tell me; are you a *Mydus`i?*"

He watched her with careful amber eyes. "A what?" she spat out. Kallie was flabbergasted. Her mind raced wildly. *Is he crazy?* But for the life of her, she couldn't understand why she felt that he was one of the sanest people she had ever met. She felt sure of him.

His mouth curved into that heart-twisting smile at her questioning look, "It seems that I must take you for what you are. No, I am not crazy." Then, as though coming to a decision, he sat beside her, his warm eyes meeting hers. Suddenly, he reached for the pendant she wore around her neck. "Where did you get this from?" Kallie drew her hand in protectively. "It was my mother's."

She replied, now hyper aware of how close they were sitting.

"Where is she now?"

Kallie paused.

"I don't know. No one knows. She disappeared after I was born. I've never met her." Her eyes clouded over as she spoke, she had never willingly disclosed anything about her mother to anyone except Hana, but now, for some reason she was telling this stranger.

But he looked like he understood how she felt, his eyes did not look at her with pity or sympathy, he just sat with her, saying nothing. He didn't feel like a stranger to Kallie and she felt strangely safe with him next to her.

For the life of him, Theo couldn't work out his feelings or thoughts; here was this mystery woman who had the most exotic aura, she could be a dangerous creature in disguise. He had heard about *Circes, Mohas* siren women who lure you deep into a fantasy world, trapping your soul forever. He knew he should be cautious but his feelings ran in an entirely different direction. He had never seen anyone so vulnerable, yet so serene. So beautiful. *She might be a wood nymph*, he mused. Her blonde hair curling softly, her striking green eyes— everything about her had that intangible quality—he wanted to catch it in his hands and never let go.

His heart went out powerfully to her, even as his mind screamed caution. Usually he was a calm, logical being with complete control over himself and everything around him. Now, it was as though a dam had burst and he was caught in the rushing rapids.

* * *

Kallie's voice cut through his thoughts, "How are you able to see halos? What are you? Why do you want to know about my research?" He looked indecisive, his old sceptical look returning. He pulled away, murmuring, "It is too dangerous, you do not want to know". And with that he vanished into the trees

Kallie sat and blinked, dumbfounded. She could not make heads or tails of this guy. He was hot then cold. Until then, she had only read about tantalizing men who could lure women with just their eyes, and now here was a man who made her breath stop just by glancing at her. She whispered after him, "Theo…" She had no doubt that he would come again. But next time, she would be ready for him.

Now, where had she heard that term *Mydus`i*?

CHAPTER FOUR

Kallie jumped in her Camaro, her mind racing with questions. She decided to bring her research notes, clippings, and everything she had connected to her current research home with her. Sour gummy bears and some reading in bed were in order; she was "sick" after all—candy was allowed. Plus it's nearly Halloween.

It had been hours since she'd arrived home, she had been through all kinds of old Magic; witches, wizards and warlocks, werewolves and lycanthropes, dwarves and yet… She could find nothing about Mydus`i. But her failure did not dissuade her. Instead, like a hunter in trail of an elusive prey, her senses tingled at the prospect of a pursuit through her other notes.

Excitement growing, she started to turn the pages on Vampyre, or Vampires as they're more commonly known in this modern era: they were the toughest to sort through and get any negligible information from, most of it being tarnished by Hollywood's new age twinkly type. Kallie sighed. She had scoured through ancient libraries finding as many fragments of actual information as she could for her thesis project months before with not much luck. Her eyes felt dry and scratchy; she rubbed them lazily.

As she started a new book, a heavy, dust covered, leather-bound copy, *Vampyre as a species possess impossible speed.* Her eyes flew open out of their tired reverie. *Pale… charismatic… beautiful… incredibly dangerous… deadly.* He was pale, his eyes glowed amber, he was super-fast and above all, the pure sexual pull and magnetism. She read the last part again: incredibly dangerous… deadly. Her stomach clenched. I mean of course vampires are deadly! They rely on human blood to survive. Kallie's brow furrowed frustrated. Theo had made her feel… different, but not just different. He made her feel safe. Surely she had this all wrong. Her intuition can't be that terrible.

Her mind raced again; *vampires can't come out in the sun, right?* Kallie scowled, confused. Well, he'd sat in the sun with her in the park, clear as day. Also, where were his fangs? Maybe he was some sort of a half vampire mix, enabling him to wander under the sun.

Do those even exist?

But Kallie was a bit cynical, she could never believe that an actual vampire would hunt her down, a mythologist professor, and give himself away. What would be the point? The risk? Assuming they even exist at all! Maybe she was going insane. She tried to unpack this chaos and find some sanity.

Myths and legends are just that,—Myths! Plus, he was asking about the transformative rituals too. So, most likely, he's just some wannabe vampire. Amber eyes? Contact lenses – easy to buy online. But the speed…?

Kallie grew frustrated. None of this made sense. She rubbed her head which currently had a marching band thumping around inside it. He looked intelligent, calm and quick witted. He didn't act like a nutcase; she sat back against her pillows and headboard, stretching, her back aching from bending over dozens of books for hours.

There was a quick rap on the door, before it was flung open.

Hana breezed in, "Hope you're decent" she sang, plopping herself heavily on Kallie's bed. "Hell, I don't know why I bother knocking. It's not like you're ever having raunchy sex in here!" Kallie threw a pillow at her as Hana laughed. "If you don't get away from your books soon, the only thing making love to you will be the laptop."

"Always so mean!" Kallie shot back sarcastically as Hana chuckled.

Hana was just like that—irreverent and funny. She was a happy-go-lucky girl, with a lot of spunk and determination. For the past few years, she had been determined to have the time of her life trying to find out what she really loved; to find her passion. She flitted from job to job, making her a jack-of-all-trades. Kallie sometimes worried about her, but she knew better than to advise, Hana wasn't one to take guidance and she knew that she would find her footing in her own time. Hana knew Kallie worried about her too; but she wanted to do her own thing, not what everyone else thought she should do.

In almost everything, they were polar opposites. It's a wonder they'd stuck together for so long. Kallie knew how most friendships ended in people drifting apart over the years. Their viewpoint may be different, but their basic principles were the same: loyalty, love, and respect. They both appreciated the other's views and only wanted what was best for each other. Whenever they fought they always made up soon after, hashing out their problems and hugging it out.

Hana worried about Kallie too. Sometimes, she felt like going the extra mile in her resignation to live in the moment, just to compensate for Kallie's lack of interest for adventure. Hana wanted Kallie to stop focusing so much on her mythological research and start living her life. After all, you're only young once. You can't live your life through fiction! She also wisely suspected that Kallie was trying to get closer to her parents, specifically her Mom, through the only link she has: history.

Hana knew that nothing could ever make up for the loss of Kallie's mother. But, try as they might, they could never find any mention of her anywhere. It all became too difficult and they eventually called it quits. It was as though she never even existed. Hana herself was a very practical person, and definitely didn't believe in myths and legends.

Hana looked over at Kallie, something felt different about her; she looked tired, but excitement danced behind her eyes, a small fire brewed. "What is the matter, babes? Found a unicorn?" Hana wiggled her eyebrows and smirked. Kallie smiled mischievously, "Something like that." Then, seeing Hana's astonished look, Kallie proceeded to tell her about the events of the past two days.

* * *

Hana stared at Kallie "Wait… you are saying that he might be a vampire?" Hana laughed bouncing in her seat "Wow, is he as hot as that British guy in the movies? Did you see any friends of his lurking in the background?" Kallie picked up a large fluffy pillow to throw at her. Hana ducked laughing and said; "But why all this fucking around business? If he is actually a "vampire", Hana's fingers making quotations in the air, "then can't he just mesmerize you and suck out all the information he wants like they do in the movies? I guess that poor guy has the hots for you!" Kallie laughed out loud, "I don't even know if mesmerizing is a real thing, Hana. Movies aren't exactly reliable source material!" They both giggled.

Kallie added, "Plus, I doubt he has the hots for me, but he definitely makes me feel… different. I just can't work it out. I've never felt like this before." Hana eyed her carefully and could tell it was true, something had definitely changed. "What else happened?" Kallie flushed magenta. "There was a dream…" her hands covered her face smiling. Kallie described the whole scene, his hands on her throat, her hair, her thighs. How is eyes glowed a brilliant red. And that line: *pretty good… for a human.*

Hana whistled. "Wow, that's intense. If he makes you feel like that and helps you cut loose a little he sounds great! He does sound a bit too good to be true though…?"

Kallie frowned as she continued. "I just want you to be careful is all, but I think you should see him again for sure." Hana replied. "Plus get a photo for me to perv on!" Kallie and Hana laughed again.

With that insightful comment, Hana snatched away Kallie's notes and started to sing: "Kallie and Theo, sitting in a tree; K.I.S.S.I.N.G.!" Hana jumped up on the bed belting out that ridiculous school yard song, Kallie rushed at Hana trying to catch her, but failed miserably as they chased each other around the room. Kallie threw another pillow in Hana's direction. Damn, Hana was too quick for her. Hana smirked "Babes, you need do to some cardio. If you can't catch me, you'll never catch your vampire hottie!" Kallie blew a raspberry at Hana, they both cackled crazily and flopped back onto the bed. Kallie decided to postpone her research for the rest of the night, she was beat.

"Thanks, Hana Banana."

"Anytime, Kallie Belly."

Hana gave her a hug and got up. "Get some shut eye, but don't make 'em too steamy!" Hana winked, shooting her some finger guns before sauntering out the door. Kallie giggled and sighed, shifting her papers off the bed before sliding between her sheets; her mind drifting between vampires and Theo. Danger and excitement.

CHAPTER FIVE

Kallie woke up suddenly in the morning. She was perspiring, the nightmare still too real for her. She had been having multiple dreams lately; it was either about her and Theo in a borderline illegal sexual position or she found herself in a weird fantasy world fighting against monsters. She looked at her clock—it was four in the morning. She felt too restless to go back to sleep, instead she started pouring through her notes once again.

Time flew by; success came to her at last, after a night of frantic searching, she finally found the term *'Mydus`i'*. It was there in her scribbled notes on Vampires, by a woman who fancied herself to be a "witch". She was taking that self-proclaimed title with a grain of salt. Kallie hadn't been too sure with her as a source; she wasn't sure how trustworthy she could really be. But, when Kallie had gone back to her again to find out more, she couldn't find her.

And now, Kallie felt the world around her swirling rapidly. All that she had known was tumbling down. Her well-structured world was giving in to chaos. Until then Kallie, though a mythologist herself, never really believed that she would come into contact with an actual mythological creature. It was like believing in God. You think God exists, but you never actually believe that you will see God one day, do you? And definitely not sitting next to you on a park bench.

Now, the fantastic, elusive world wreathed in mystery was opening itself up for her, tantalising her to enter. Wild thoughts flew around her head; maybe she would start seeing Centaurs and Cyclops next she thought, a crazed giggle escaping her lips.

Kallie took a nice long bath; falling asleep in the tub, lying there in the hot water. She suddenly woke up, looking at herself in dismay. *Great, now I'm all wrinkled.* She scrubbed herself, applied a tonne of moisturizer and pulled on her favourite blue jeans, matching them with a plaid shirt and brown knee high boots. She chucked on some light makeup—*there, now I'm ready to take on the world.*

She checked through her emails and messages in her phone. There were the usual adverts, innocuous masseurs' entreaties and real estate messages. She paused at a message from an unknown number, which said, "Hello, this is Theodore. Can we meet at the coffee shop near the park at eleven in the morning tomorrow?" She looked at the time of the message. It had been sent last night but she was too distracted with Hana and the research. She checked the time on her phone, it was 10 a.m. *Shit.*

Kallie bit her lip anxiously. She did want to meet a real-life Vampire and she did want to see Theo again. But she was terrified. Still, he had never tried to hurt her in any way. Her hands started typing on their own, "Okay, sure. Can you still make it?" She hit the send button. The reply was immediate, as though she had typed it herself: A terse "yes."

Her stomach clenched as she read it, Kallie had never felt so excited and petrified in her whole life. Was she really doing this? She quickly brushed on some lip gloss, grabbed her scarf and headed out the door. It seems she was. Driving through the city streets it took her 15 minutes to reach the park. She was at the coffee shop early, which was fine by Kallie; she wanted to see how he arrived. *I wonder what kind of car he drives.* Her mind was buzzing with frantic questions. Does he drive a car...? Fly? She made herself laugh.

She was stirring her coffee mindlessly when he was suddenly standing there. *Damn it, she missed his entrance.* Theo's face was inscrutable; he didn't give away any signs to his emotions. He sat down and looked at her.

They sat in silence for a minute. Kallie felt nervous, but her courage stood in its stead. With a slight quavering voice she spoke, "I think… I know who you are" Theo merely looked at her. Kallie felt her voice growing tinier, her eyes flicked around the room quickly. She glanced back leaning forward; "…Vampire", she whispered.

Theo didn't say a thing, his poker face strong. Kallie added, "Isn't it true?" She felt a growing frustration as he held her gaze. "Well, are you going to say anything at all?" As though coming to a decision, Theo's gaze broke and he sighed, leaning forward to match her and spoke quietly "Yes, I am indeed what you call me." Kallie looked at him in wonder, eyes widening, wringing her hands nervously. She wasn't only nervous about her suspicions being correct but being in the presence of Theo again.

Kallie opened her mouth, closed it, and then she opened it once again. Theo asked, "Are you going to keep imitating a goldfish or are you going to ask me something?" She felt herself blushing and asked abruptly, "Can I ask you some questions? Please? I've never met a… well, anything like you…" Kallie trailed off looking at her hands. She didn't want to sound stupid. She was a mythology professor but there was clearly so much she didn't know. Theo was dead still, staring again, "You may." he stated.

"Do vampires speak either in monosyllables or in sarcastic outpourings?" She queried with a slight smile, startled by her own brashness. Theo's lips tilted slightly. Kallie smiled back with relief. "Okay, I'll start with my first question: If you're really a vampire, can't you just use mind control on me? Isn't that supposed to be your specialty?"

Theo looked at her pensively and replied "I also cannot figure that out. It has never happened to me before. For some reason my powers don't affect you."

Kallie's surprise was growing. So he does have powers. "So I'm the only person you can't… control?" Kallie countered. Theo lips tugged again, amused. "I suppose."

Kallie continued quickly, "But you can wander in daylight… Are you only half-vampire? Why does the sun not affect you? Where are your fangs?" Kallie looked flushed, with her eyes twinkling and a smile lifting the corners of her lips. She felt like she needed a pen and paper to take notes. Theo couldn't help himself from smiling. That was the first time Kallie saw him smile a smile that wasn't sarcastic or mirthless in nature, it somehow transformed him. It was as though, the veils and walls around him dropped, she felt it pull her heartstrings in a strange way; and he still looked irresistibly sexy.

He asked "If I satisfy your curiosity, will you give me the information I seek?" Kallie nodded quickly. Theo answered, "The saying that Vampires do not come out in daylight was a myth created by our kind to protect ourselves. The days of persecution… execution, people pestering us for everlasting life and youth. It made us crave privacy. It is useful in luring prey too, they don't expect us to be out in the daytime" He smirked wildly.

Kallie's eyes flickered, wide. "Do you drink human blood?" Theo looked irritated, "Do all humans eat meat? No, there are vegetarians among us. Like humans choosing their diet, we do also. Human blood is not needed to survive, animal blood will suffice, but it comes with strong cravings, which can, and must be controlled. But it can be difficult."

Kallie didn't hide her relief. "What about your fangs? Is that a myth too?" Theo smiled once again, oh how sexy he looked! Kallie felt her mind wandering into dangerous zones again. She forced herself to gain control, snapping back to reality.

His smile grew mocking, as though he could read that thought too. But, he just said, "No, we do have fangs. But they are hidden by magic, so as not to scare the ahhh… prey" his hand gesturing as he said the word. "Can I… see them?" Kallie pleaded.

Theo felt his heart flutter watching Kallie grow intrigued with him, he knew he should stop but couldn't. "I'm sorry, it's not safe here."

Kallie was disappointed but continued. "But how have you not become the superior race? With your strength and speed, you could have easily overthrown humans!"

Theo replied, "Just like any other creatures we have our own covens, strengths and weaknesses. We just want to exist peacefully and be left to our own devices. Vampires are a secluded group. Everlasting life can actually become quite wearisome. That is why…" He stopped, brow furrowed as he looked out the window behind her. Kallie watched him, her eyes full of compassion and understanding.

He began again, "I have been searching for many years to find a way to reverse the curse. I wish to be human again. My searching led me to you, Kallie." He sighed, shifting in his seat. It was the first time Kallie had seen him look vulnerable, even a little insignificant. It was as though a great weight had been lifted off his shoulders by sharing his burden with her.

Kallie didn't say: "Being a vampire must be amazing! All that strength and immortality... Are you kidding me?" She somehow understood his feelings. Being immortal; all your friends and family slowly dying around you. It must be awful, not to mention lonely. She pried gently, "How old are you? I mean how old are you really?" Theo remained pensive. She continued, "I did hear about a ritual in my research, but the woman who told me about it wasn't there the next time I visited. It was near the Bash Bish falls, it's a small village near Mt. Washington. I'd have to look through my notes again and work out the exact location..." Kallie trailed off fumbling, unsure of what to say next.

Theo looked relieved; finally here was someone who didn't insist on arguing with him about his plan. He looked at her speculatively, "Please. It would be great if you could get me the details." Kallie agreed "If I get you the village name, will you tell me more about yourself? Who you were? Do you really transform into bats? I have so many questions." Theo's mouth crinkled adorably. "I will" She loved to see him smile again. "Then please, can I see your fangs!" Kallie tried again, eyes twinkling.

Theo looked around slowly in consideration; she was smiling mischievously. Theo felt something breaking inside him, as he looked at her glowing hair, her impish smile and her beautiful, green eyes. He softened and then drew close to her, so that it looked like they were almost kissing. He was holding her head. Kallie felt herself swoon slightly at being so close to Theo again. He opened his mouth, whispered something quickly and his fangs were visible. They looked so sharp and dare she say it, sexy as hell. He looked into her eyes and longed to kiss her. He murmured something and they vanished as he swiftly sat back in his chair.

Kallie snapped back to the present, breathless at the loss of his touch. She was dying for that kiss to happen. The dream dancing in her mind again; teasing her. They looked at each other, the fire palpable between them.

Theo said, "Same place, tomorrow evening at five then?" Kallie nodded, and with that, he left. Kallie remained sitting in her chair for a long time, her coffee untouched.

CHAPTER SIX

Screams and bangs rendered the air apart. Initially, he had thought it was a macabre scene enacted from a drama. His mother lay dying on the steps, while his father and brother lay dead at the dining table, fallen halfway from the chairs. The screaming he had heard on his way up had died by that time. He knew that Margot and June were no more. He felt paralysed with pain. Then he heard a rushing sound from behind. He knew intuitively, it was too late for him too…

His memories were always evergreen, the hurt in his eyes remained the same, after hundreds of years and he still never got used to the pain. He is usually so good at suppressing memories, but after meeting Kallie he couldn't quash anything anymore—something about her smile and warmth reminded him of home too often.

* * *

After work the next day Kallie returned to her apartment and started shifting her books and clearing her desk, tidying absent-mindedly—everything felt strange to her. Everything had changed and cleaning just seemed trivial. She was seeing the world with a new set of eyes. How she wished she could share this with her Grandmother. She had always said, "This world is big enough for all sorts of creatures to dwell in, beyond our sight. Just because we can't see the radio and TV waves, it doesn't mean they don't exist. We just need to discover a new way to see them, with open eyes and heart."

How right she was! She proudly thought that her Grandma would have liked Theo. She flushed. Here she was, thinking about how her grandma would like a man about whom she knew nothing about. She felt childish, like a sixteen year old wishing her family would like her new boyfriend… Hell!

Why was she even thinking like that?!

She had a new energy which had been missing in her for the past few years, due to her research she could not sit still—she started tidying up her room, trivial yes but still necessary.

Suddenly it was four o'clock. Just one more hour until she sees Theo again, her stomach clenched at the thought. She looked a mess and started to clean herself up. She felt light-hearted and giddy with anticipation as she gathered all her precious research materials into her bag. Kallie grabbed a denim jacket and her keys before locking up.

Kallie walked into the coffee-shop with butterflies in her stomach that made her aware of so many things she had never noticed before. She could feel the light hilly breeze bringing in the soft sent of pines, the clarity of her vision, her sense of smell, her hearing. It all seemed to be in over-drive. She had never felt that way before and it scared and thrilled her at the same time.

Theo was at the café already, sitting in one of the spots with couches by the window. He was in dark blue jeans this time, a tidy black belt with silver buckle and plain black shirt, collar slightly open. Kallie's eyes caught sight of his chest and felt her face glow red. He felt her presence before seeing her, turning in his seat at the café entrance to lock eyes with hers.

When their eyes met, Kallie felt the world going hot and sparks flying. *I feel like a damn teenager with hormonal overdrive!!* Kallie mused with a wry smile, blushing. She made her way towards him, careful to avoid looking at him so he wouldn't see her rouged face.

* * *

Theo noticed. He knew the effects of his vampire powers, whereas earlier he would have just shrugged it off with a sly smile, but this girl was different. His powers had no effect on Kallie and whatever she felt was all her own. This, for the first time, made Theo nervous.

Though he desperately wanted to focus on his quest, he could not help feeling distracted by all this upsurge of emotions and conflict inside him, he knew his blood flow had long ceased, his heart had stopped beating precisely 152 years ago. But looking at Kallie made him feel hot and cold at the same time, with a roaring sound in his ears. He knew that it was all due to his brain going haywire and firing on all cylinders. Of all the people to rouse him out of his fevered search, it had to be the one person who was the final key to his quest!

Kallie sat in her chair, placed her laptop on the table and busied herself with starting it up and finding the relevant files for Theo. She had jotted down the various points of interest in her computer as she browsed through her piles of old manuscripts, interviews and notes. Theo felt his impatience growing and started to pull the laptop towards him, she shooed his hands off with a light slap, Theo laughed at the thought of a human trying to shoo him away.

The waitress arrived with a seductive smile, batting her eyelashes in Theo's direction "What would you like today?" He barely noticed, keeping his eyes on Kallie. "Uh, I'll have a coffee and blueberry muffin" Kallie replied with a smile. "Nothing for me" Theo finally countered. The waitress scowled at Kallie enviously tossing her hair around, as though she had insulted her with such a measly order and sauntered off.

Kallie laughed lightly amused, eyeing Theo who also had a smirk on his face. She turned back to her laptop, opening the related documents on vampire transformation ritual, this time, he asked, "May I have your laptop now?" She smiled as she passed it on to him, he scrolled through the document and other files in a blur; it was as though he was scanning them, then, he stopped and smiled at her. "You have done an amazing job. I have never seen anyone be so thorough in gathering evidence and supporting materials. You have even organized them perfectly. You have clearly worked hard on this."

Kallie glowed at his comment, it felt great to hear him praising instead of passing some sarcastic comments.

So he was nice too…

Theo was saying, "I never knew there was so much to us, I mean. It will take me days to go through your work." The waitress was back with their order which she placed with a slight thump on the table. Theo glanced at the spilt coffee and then locked eyes with the waitress with a slight smile. She blushed and smiled back at him "I'm so sorry I'll get you another," she walked away with the slopped coffee in a daze. He turned back towards Kallie seeming annoyed at the waitress' interruption and said, "If you don't mind, can we finish this in my apartment? It will be more practical and… private. Unless you are opposed to the idea?"

Kallie looked uncertain; her mind said, *Alone in an apartment, with a vampire?? Kallie are you going nuts?* While her body and womanly parts said *GO, GO, GO!* She instinctively believed that he would never harm her. She decided to go with her gut. Theo added solemnly, "I promise to be on my best behaviour" with a wink. Kallie blushed, for the millionth time today; her face might actually be stuck a shade of fuchsia at this rate. "Ok." She agreed, "Let's go."

Leaving their coffees and with Theo leaving their terrible waitress a large tip, they walked into the sunshine. She felt a shuddering thrill inside her; here she was, going off into the unknown territory of which she had only read about, but never seen; with a creature she herself had thought belonged only in fantasy.

* * *

Theo had thought his journey would've come to an end when he found the ritual but he'd never bargained on Kallie, she changes everything. He wanted to shrug all his emotions away and concentrate only on the ritual, but he couldn't bring himself to. The thought of wrenching himself away from her nearly caused him physical pain.

This is stupid! This is stupid and unbelievably dangerous! He should have stolen her research and ran. *Why am I letting myself go crazy over a woman like this? It would be best to take away her work and erase her memory.* But seeing how she had poured her life into her research, he felt guilty to even think about stealing it. And his powers also don't work on her even if he wanted to.

Theo had to admit that her ingenuity in searching for materials, following up the clues and relentless research had resulted in a unique insight into the world of vampires and other creatures he had seen in his life.

She stopped at the parking lot and asked nervously, "Ah, did you come by car?" Theo smiled sardonically, "Is that a question to ask a vampire?" Kallie replied coolly, "We'll take my car then", rolling her eyes.

"Let me drive, it will be much faster", Theo said, slipping into the driver's seat. Kallie paused, cautioning. She never let anyone else drive The Camaro. She finally handed Theo the keys, "Fine, but don't scratch her!"

He drove them from the park towards a more secluded part of town where the people valued their privacy and peace. Lots of trees lined the roads and the apartment blocks were few and far between. They stopped by a discreet apartment designed like a colonial piece of building; it was a tribute to the solidity and elegance of its time.

Kallie had imagined a large castle or mansion, dark and looming. Movie clichés were hard to break. *This is interesting.* They walked through the front door into a foyer with minimal décor. Light grey walls and two potted plants flanked a non-descript elevator door. They stepped inside and he pushed the button for the highest floor, number 15. There hardly seemed to be anyone else in the whole apartment block. If anything happened, she was sure, no one would know. The door chimed and Theo stepped through gesturing for her to follow, welcoming her with his trademark smile.

"Welcome to my home".

CHAPTER SEVEN

Kallie looked around his apartment with mounting interest, the apartment was spacious, full of light and air, the furniture was solid and comfortable, made of old wood and luscious fabrics. The lounge and kitchen were all open plan with beautiful pieces of contemporary art gracing the walls. "So... vampires prefer a more real estate magazine vibe than medieval dungeon, castle feel?" she noted with a nervous giggle.

Theo raised his eyebrows with a slight smile and then shrugged. "Depends on the vampire I suppose." He plugged in her laptop and started going through her materials on the large, charcoal sofa. Kallie took out her old interview notes, sitting next to Theo and started going through them. She glanced up at him as they worked; getting distracted. He began rolling the sleeves on his shirt up and her mind immediately recalled his hand on her face yesterday. Kallie flicked her eyes away quickly, shaking her head. She needed to focus. She looked back down at her notes. She felt that she had missed something the first time she had read through these and it kept nagging at her. But try as she might, she couldn't remember what it was. Kallie felt frustrated and threw her notes aside. She felt tired and hungry. She glanced at her phone; it was nearly midnight!

Kallie felt that if she stayed any longer, she might become a midnight snack herself. She wondered how she could leave, without disturbing Theo who looked as though he had disappeared into her computer. She touched his arm lightly, "I think I need to head home, get some sleep. Humans need to ahh, sleep…" Kallie said jokingly, "I can come back tomorrow, if you like?"

Theo shook himself and said, "Forgive me; I have been a bad host. I forget how quickly time can disappear. You must be hungry. I feel the need for a snack myself." He smiled as he talked, baring his teeth slightly. Kallie felt goose bumps rising on her skin, though she managed an "Okay, sure, that would be great." With a blink of an eye, Theo returned with a tray of sandwiches and hot coffee.

She bit into them ravenously as Theo watched her. She asked, "What about you?" He smiled one again. "I will do my hunting later; I want to read more. Will you leave your laptop with me?" Kallie hesitated; "Don't worry. I won't delete anything. I just need time to copy them over."

Kallie nodded "I'll be back by 9 then." Both Kallie and Theo stood up. Theo looked into her eyes and said, "I can't thank you enough for what you have done. This research… It means more than you know." His eyes grew darker as he spoke; Kallie felt her insides turning to mush; she wanted to grow roots and stay there, at that place forever, staring into his eyes.

She croaked out an "it's nothing; glad to help" and went to the door shakily. Theo looked at her with concern," Are you alright? Shall I come with you?" With a disgruntled, "I wish", echoing in her mind, Kallie refused his offer and went down to her car. She exhaled deeply putting her head against her steering wheel. His parting words and the look in his eyes engulfed her.

Wow. She kept saying to herself as she cruised her car through the town as though in a dream.

Kallie woke up early, too excited to sleep. After showering she decided on a cashmere sweater in mustard, a flowing maroon skirt that stopped at her thighs and suede knee high boots. She eyed herself in the floor length mirror, turning side to side. A long gold moon pendant and she was done. She normally wouldn't wear something so short but she wanted to make an impression.

She pressed the buzzer for Theo's door waiting to be let inside. She glanced at the other floors windows and noticed that most of them had the curtains drawn. *Strange.* The lock clicked, she opened the door and walked inside. She reached the top floor. Ding! The doors opened and there he was; he looked as fresh as ever, nothing to suggest that he was going without sleep. *Oh, to not need to sleep, the things she'd get done!*

He smiled at her; he was still in a shirt but this one was plaid. He wore it open with a white t-shirt underneath. Light blue jeans, his dark hair messy in a very sexy way. He looked amazing.

Kallie spied an oil painting by the fireplace; she went over to have a closer look. It showed a family of six: two parents, two brothers and two sisters. One of them looked like Theo, a very young Theo. He was watching her; she looked at him with the tentative question in her eyes.

His lips grew tight. It looked as though he was going to dismiss the question; instead, he closed his eyes and began his story.

His father was a respected landowner in New England; their father's family was quite large with lots of uncles and cousins. It was a close knit place. His mother was graceful and beautiful. Her kindness and firm upbringing was stamped in all of them: his brother Sebastian, himself, his twin sisters Margot and June. Sebastian took care of running the family antiquities business, while he, Theo, went on roaming far and high, in search of the rare and elusive for them to sell.

It was from one such travel that he was returning from, when his life changed forever. It was 1892, Theo was 25 when he had received a letter from Sebastian saying that a mysterious illness was plaguing their town. It was an event that historians would now call the New England Vampire Panic, but we were many years away from that. Villagers were dying and some even disappearing without a trace. Many of their cousins had died. Even their uncle, William Barlow was missing. Everyone had lost someone and villagers had begun fleeing the town as a last resort.

Theo had finally returned home after rushing back to witness his whole family perish before his eyes. Uncle William, once so full of charm and pranks, had gone on a bloody rampage, leaving everyone dead. Theo fought with him and was bitten, William then forced him to turn by drinking his blood and then killing him. When we awoke, William was gone. "I resented living when everyone I loved had died. Why would he bother turning me at all? It would have been kinder to have died along with them. I hurt a lot of people… killed a lot of people in those early years. The blood lust is so strong when you are reborn. It drove me crazy I disappeared into the mountains. I came back only after controlling myself completely. My uncle was never seen again after that night."

Kallie was devastated, she never imagined anything like this, and she could see the pain and sorrow in his eyes. He had a strong exterior but Kallie could tell this memory cut him deeply. Theo didn't say anything; he stared at the portrait for a moment longer before returning to the sofa. Kallie felt a tear escape and roll down her cheek. She quickly wiped it away before following him. She knew that he didn't want any words of consolation. What could she say? The silence between them was prolonged, though tinged with melancholy.

After some time, Theo asked Kallie, "Do you know anything about werewolves and other beings?" Kallie was glad for the change of topic, she told him about what she could find: "As far as I can see, werewolves are just a species related to humans that never died out. I really think they have a gene mutation that enhances their wolf-like abilities. Just like the myth about vampires not coming out in the sun, the story about changing on a full moon must be a myth they use to protect themselves. Have you interacted with any?"

"Yes, I have. There is a local spot they like to meet; they are one of the most secretive, mistrustful creatures." Kallie was surprised to hear that another creature she thought was fiction was indeed factual. "Do you mind if I make a coffee?" She asked.

"Of course, be my guest" Theo smiled.

Kallie wandered to the kitchen, as she was hunting for a coffee pot she instead came across a very fancy, very large barista quality coffee machine. *Uhhh.* Suddenly, he was there, behind her; "Do you need a hand?" She gave out a breathless "yes…". His hand shot out above her head, his body pressing close to hers, pulling down a container with what looked like coffee beans, he sat it next to the machine. "Sugar…?" She turned around, her eyes meeting his, her whole body felt on fire. Her innards were starting to go haywire with anticipation and desire. She sighed out another "yes". He placed it next to the first container, his muscular arms resting either side of her on the kitchen bench.

Kallie swooned as her breathing hitched in her throat. Visions of her dream came flooding back to her. Theo pressed in closer, the button on his jeans hitting her crotch as he ran his hand up the nape of her neck and into her hair. He leans in, his amber eyes locked with hers and he stops just before their lips meet, "we shouldn't…" Theo whispers. "I know" she replies. Finally his lips hit hers and it feels like fire, Kallie's body shudders as long-held lust and desire courses through her veins. Their kissing starts slow and then builds, passion takes over. Her stomach contracts; her whole body tuned tightly to his touch and caresses. Everything around them dissolves into nothing but pure need. Her senses were on overload. She could feel him through every tiny hair on her skin.

Theo groaned and pulled her tight towards him, as though he had been hungry since forever. His hands ran over her breasts, the gentle swell of her hips, he pulled her closer with urgency, in a single fluid movement; he pulled off her short skirt and sweater, leaving her in nothing but boots. He threw off his shirt revealing his defined torso, she became breathless and her hands moved of their own accord down his chest. She reached for his clothes, his belt, and started unbuttoning his pants.

Theo lifted her, just as she wrapped her long legs around his hips. He looked intently into her eyes, as though trying to read her. She smiled lightly, moaned and pulled him inside her, with her legs on the kitchen island and seated at the counter. Kallie's office dream came flooding back to her, clenching her insides deliciously. Theo embraced her fiercely and they started moving together slowly, in perfect sync, like they were the only two people in the world. It was as though the waves kept coming inside her. Theo looked at her closed eyes, her parted lips as she tilted her head back in pleasure and it was all he could do to stop from biting her. He had never been with a human in all his years as a vampire and he wanted her badly, rough and urgent, but he felt the need to take things slower, to let her feel him, in new ways no one else had. It made him feel warm watching her reach for his body like she did.

He was not always a man to share sexual control and power; he was dominant in the real sense of the word. It excited him to know and see how much control he had and how much his woman wanted to please him.

But Kallie was different, she was delicate and Theo would never forgive himself if he hurt her. For now this was enough, he didn't want to scare her.

Kallie's nails dug into his back, moaning as she reached her climax, her lips next to his ear as he thrust deeply inside her. Theo leaned on her, his heaviness a delicious burden, they were slick with sweat breathing heavily; Kallie felt as though she was born again; the whole world felt different, she held on to him tightly her body shaking, he lifted her gently from the counter, with her unsteady legs still wrapped around him, and carried her to his bedroom.

It was an old-fashioned four poster bed with soft pillows and pristine sheets. Theo placed her on the bed lightly, unzipping her boots before sliding in next to her. She still couldn't believe it, this felt much better than any of her dreams, and the intensity when he touched her… she could see him try to control himself, see him try to hold himself in, was he scared he'd hurt her? Did he think she couldn't handle him in his glory? Questions swirled through her mind, and in a minute it was a hazy blur, she could not think of anything more than the feel of his hands on her body, his touch, and how it made her feel.

Theo was unexpectedly gentle, as though she were a fragile flower that could be crushed in his hands. He ran his fingers through her golden hair, and touched his lips to hers, the line of her jaw, her high cheekbones, the line of her forehead, as though trying to memorize them. He gazed at her, the aura around her glowed, a muted yellowy orange like the setting sun, faintly lighting the pillow around her head.

He murmured, "I have never seen your halo like this, it has always been a golden colour, but now it's more orange, like fire."

Kallie sat up slightly, trying to understand what he was saying.

"What halo?"

"Haven't you come across this in your research? "He asked.

"No. What is it?"

"Everyone has one. Normal humans have a halo, or aura, of a reddish-brown/grey colour. I don't know what each colour of the aura means, but reds are usually associated with stronger people. I had never seen a golden aura before meeting you." Theo explained.

"But why should mine be any different?" She asked puzzled. "Are you sure you are human? I can't control your emotions like other humans." Kallie laughed "As far as I know, I'm a boring, normal human. I was an average student, played games and read books. My dad was always busy with his work and grandma was there for me when he couldn't…"

"Your mother? I'm sure she must be a remarkable person." Theo countered.

Kallie smiled, "How do you know?" Theo replied with a smile, "Just my instinct".

"I don't know anything about my mother, except her name. I don't even have any pictures of her. When I asked my dad about it, he just said that she never liked having her pictures taken."

"What did your dad say about it?"

"Dad defended her, saying that her circumstances were very difficult, but that she loved me deeply. This was all she left me." Kallie replied, holding the rowan wood pendant around her neck. Eyes dimming as she reminisced about her mother. Theo was intrigued, but decided to pursue it later. He pulled her into him and held her close.

CHAPTER EIGHT

"I can't believe I haven't met him yet!" Hana exclaimed while they had breakfast. Kallie smiled, "I know, Han, soon I promise!" It had been a month since that night in Theo's apartment and they were spending more and more time together, researching for more clues about the ritual, amongst other things…

"We should all do something amazing for Halloween!" Hana replied as she took another bite of toast. "That's such a good idea! I really want you two to meet. I think you'll like him." Kallie grinned again. "Well you're looking amazing, I think he's good for you" Hana said.

Hana was right; she couldn't imagine her world without Theo. She had never felt better, her skin glowed, her hair shone and she felt radiant. She just didn't know how to break it to her best friend that Theo was actually a vampire! Yes they'd joked about it but now it's a legitimate reality and she didn't want to put Hana in harm's way. Plus Theo probably wouldn't be pleased if another human new his secret. It had been playing on her mind and she found it difficult to concentrate at work, but luckily for Kallie the winter break was fast approaching and she could relax a bit. She had a few things start to accumulate at Theo's, a spare toothbrush, her shampoo and conditioner, some lingerie, she was at his place more than her own. Luckily Hana was an understanding best friend and housemate, even though she had been marginally avoiding her so as to avoid to "vampire" topic.

Theo and Kallie had been researching for so long now; days and nights spent hunched over laptops and books. They couldn't seem to find the last piece of the puzzle. She could see Theo growing frustrated and Kallie had tried to change Theo's mind on numerous occasions, to talk him into finally accepting his truth, "Theo, I love you for who you are, for all the things that make you, you. We don't know how the ritual works or if it truly even exists!" But he was adamant about continuing.

"I didn't ask for this life. I want to live a full, normal human life with you."

Kallie knew that whatever she said, he would never change his mind. Not on this topic. She wondered what Hana, or her professors, would make of her now, and she was usually the sane one, the calm rational person, but she also knew that however the situation had played out; she would have always fallen for Theo.

They were still doing their research one late October evening, when it became noticeably chilly. Theo seemed unaffected by this. Of course, what was she thinking, he was a fucking vampire and she had only worn a blouse and a pair of jeans. "Do you have any heaters in here?" Kallie asked rubbing her arms.

"I don't have any use for one, but wait…"

He was there and the next minute, the fireplace was crackling with a merry log fire. He drew the couch towards the fire in a flash, as Kallie felt the warmth spread through her body. Kallie smiled; how she'd miss his super speed when he was turned back to human.

"Thanks" she said as she slowly warmed her hands against the orange flames.

Theo started to circle her shoulders with his thumb, rubbing her back and neck sensually. Kallie sighed happily as he moved next to her, his eyes burning with intensity. He ran his fingers lightly over her lips and throat. He grabbed her hair, not too roughly but just enough, and pulled her head back, till her throat shone white in the blazing fire light. He started kissing her throat, gentle at first. His mouth ran over her delicate shoulders, as his hands were whipping away her shirt and his with burning need. His hands cupped her breasts and started squeezing them, feeling her nipples grow tight. He licked her breasts, her nipples, biting with his lips. A moan escaped her parted lips; she pushed him off, down to the floor onto a thick rug. She lowered herself onto him, scrunching up her skirt, pulling his pants off deftly. Her lips met his as her whole body trembled. His hands ran all along her back, feeling her rear, her breasts. She slid himself inside her as she lowered herself down, a moan escaping them both.

The fire blazed, crackling wildly as they went, furious, their hands fighting for each other, grabbing, biting, every touch was exquisite, every thrust felt glorious. She finally lay on him, both of them spent. She knew already that there was more to Theo. She wanted him to trust her to handle all of him, but she wanted him to do it in his own time. They had made love so many times now she had lost count, every day mingling insensibly as they kept working together; they were both caught up with materials, books and stories, every day, week, month they grew fonder of each other, trying to get work done, becoming distracted more often than not. Every nook and corner of his house started to have memories for Kallie: the glorious four poster bed, his couch, the fireplace; the bathrooms and even the staircase to the bedroom, it felt like home to her, she had become overly familiar with this new world.

The next day they were nearly through all of Kallie's resources when at last their luck struck, they had started pouring through an ancient book full of obscure spells, writing in a mix of tongues like Latin and ancient English. It was hard to translate and very dry to read. Luckily they could translate enough to read about a transformative spell that had to be performed on All Hallows Eve. It required a witch or wizard well versed in the tongues.

"This could be it, Kallie!" Theo exclaimed.

She'd never seen him this enthusiastic, and she was worried it might all fall through. "Please don't get your hopes up okay" Kallie replied, "We need to double check this first."

"There is a witch, Morgana. She can do this." He was certain. Many members in his realm had spoken about her. She was an ancient one who lived deep in the woods of Freetown, Fall River State Forest. Kallie had heard about the forest which was rumoured to be haunted with numerous deaths, UFO sightings and other unnatural occurrences. The supernatural seemed to call to the forest.

She'd asked Theo about it earlier. "Well, when you choose to ignore magical creatures like us, you have to invent something right? Extra-terrestrials are much more believable for people than vampires." He shrugged.

* * *

They decided to meet with Morgana and gather more information; Kallie prayed this wasn't a wild goose chase. They jumped in the car ready for a two hour drive away from the city. Kallie grabbed the book with the Latin scrawlings, she was apprehensive of what they might find, about what it would mean for Theo and her. Right then, Kallie's phone buzzed, it was Hana.

"Hey, Han."

"Kallie, where are you? I'm getting worried." Kallie didn't know what to reply. She had never hidden anything from Hana but how could she possibly explain her situation right now, she would never believe her!

"I'm fine, everything's ok… I'm with Theo."

"I'm glad you guys hooked up but you've been spending a heap of time together, I just hope you're not moving too fast…" Hana replied, worry tingeing her voice. "Its fine Hana, we're just going for a little road trip for a few days, that's all."

"Really…? Why?" Hana replied. Kallie looked anxiously at Theo knowing he could hear the whole conversation. His eyes met hers and he nodded, but pressed his lips tight together, holding the steering wheel firmly.

"Umm, actually Hana, remember the discussion we had… about Theo… that he might be a vampire? Well, turns out its true; he is one!" Kallie replied quickly with a nervous laugh, trying to lighten the situation.

Hana laughed loudly. "Ha! That's great, funny, *very* funny." She retorted sarcastically. "No seriously, what are you guys doing on a road trip and why wasn't I invited?"

Silence filled the line.

"I'm serious Hana…" Kallie countered back gently. Hana went quiet before answering; "You what now? You're seriously canoodling with a vampire! Like a blood thirsty, eats your neck, controls your mind kinda vampire…?! And you're in a car, alone, going on some sort of weird camping trip…? Are you completely insane?!"

Kallie could imagine Hana going visibly crazy in her mind; she would give everything to see the look on her best friend's face at this moment.

"You have to trust me on this Hana, this is as real as it gets."

Hana whispered into the mouth piece "Are you sure he hasn't done anything to you?! Kallie say 'pineapple' if he's kidnapped you and you need saving! I'll come right now! Pineapple…? Kallie…?"

Kallie chuckled lightly, "Honestly it's fine, amazing even. I'm sorry I had to hide this for so long. Please don't be mad, we had to. We'll talk when I'm back"

"If he hurts you, *I swear to god!*"

"I'm sorry Han, I have to go."

Kallie hung up, leaving Hana spiralling. Her phone instantly buzzed again, Hana calling back. Kallie turned her phone off miserably.

Theo exhaled and put his hand on hers, "She'll be ok; we will talk with her when we return." Kallie smiled weakly at him; "I hope so, she's my oldest friend. I can't lose her, Theo." Kallie leaned her head against the car window, watching the trees fly past. She felt so guilty for shutting Hana out of her life, she should've told her sooner. What if this ritual all goes wrong and she doesn't even get to meet Theo?

They drove for what felt like days until Theo said, "I think we've come to the end of our journey, Morgana's house is somewhere deep in this part of the woods. The trail is narrow so unfortunately from here we have to go on foot. Will you be alright?"

Kallie opened the car door, breathing in deeply. The pine-scented air seemed to revive her spirits somehow. Kallie was surprised to feel at peace when her emotions were so racked after her phone call with Hana.

"I'll be ok." She replied caressing a hand along his jaw.

The deeper they went into the forest; the happier she felt. A positive radiance danced around her and she even forgot her phone call with Hana for a while. Even the forest seemed brighter and cheerful. The birds were very noisy, chirping, flying over their heads, while a few rabbits, foxes and even squirrels started peeping out from around the brush, eager to look at the new visitors. Theo whistled. "Look at that. Usually, the forest goes dead silent whenever a vampire is around; they can sense the presence of a predator. I think they're looking at you Kallie…" Kallie beamed, astonished at all the forest creatures that had turned up.

"Oh, I don't think they're here for me." She said hesitantly. But even as she said it, Kallie watched as more animals peeped around the trees at her and wondered if Theo may be right.

But why…

They walked on and the trail turned sharply, a small spindly cottage suddenly coming into view far away in the distance. Kallie and Theo looked at each other and nodded. They clasped hands and pressed on, eager for answers.

CHAPTER NINE

The cottage was further than it looked but the woods were calm and glorious. Kallie had never seen anything this beautiful. It felt like a part of her belonged here, something felt very familiar and safe; and although it made no sense to her she didn't bother trying to figure it out, or make sense of anything. All she wanted right now was to enjoy the moment. For whatever reason, these woods had a very soothing effect on her, and that was all that mattered.

The flowers started to bloom with wild colours. The longer they walked into the woods, the more it unfolded in all its glory, welcoming them. Theo knew too well this was a sign. He had lived for too long in this world to not get the message, but it was not clear enough, the woods would not light up to a vampire—this reception had to be for Kallie, the thought of it made the hair on his skin stand on end. He knew for a fact she had told him all she knew. He trusted her, trusted her innocence, but he sensed there was more to this woman, and every day with her he was becoming even surer of this.

"This doesn't happen for regular people." he told her, noticing the sparks light up in her eyes as she witnessed the woods. Actually, he thought, this had never happened with him before.

"What?" she asked mindlessly, still basking in awe of her environment.

"Those woods are normally dull and gloomy until one of
its own walks through." He continued with his
explanation, not that he thought it would make any sense
to her.

"I don't get it." she cut in almost before the last words
could roll off his tongue.

"I don't understand either, but there really is more to
this. Listen Kallie, don't touch anything, and do not get
carried away by all this beauty, just stay next to me." His
request was simple but full of worry, it was either
something or someone here wanted to enchant Kallie or
she belonged here. The latter was very unlikely but he
didn't want to think of just the negative possibility. He
played a lot of scenes in his head and they just didn't
seem right. Whatever the case he was responsible for
bringing her here, and he would do everything he could
to keep her from harm. Not just out of obligation, but out
of love.

They walked a few miles south of the woods, there was a
fountain ahead of them, the water flowing rich, green
with life; it was an emerald sea. Kallie was even more
than fascinated. Butterflies started to fly over their
heads; they were nothing like any butterflies Kallie had
ever seen. Their wings were made of solid gold, and
when they flapped they produced sweet, lilting melodies
that warmed her heart. She regarded Theo for a while,
her eyes lingering on his taut body as he moved swiftly
next to her, the expression on his face looked nothing
like what she expected— if he had any pleasure in all
they were witnessing he did a pretty good job hiding it.
He looked worried, his face rumpled in a frown. She
wanted to reach out to him, to assure him that everything

is fine. She knew he was tense because of this visit—this meeting would define the next phase of his life for him.

They approached some sort of portal; the pathway in front of them had powerful waves, the energy so powerful it was visible. Kallie knew it was a portal, she had seen too many movies not to at least tell that stepping too close to that barrier would lead them to another destination, one she was not willing to find out.

"Don't come too close." Theo warned, an arm held protectively in front of her.

"I don't plan to."

"This isn't where we're supposed to be, I knew something was wrong. Stay here and don't take another step." He walked a few steps closer to the barrier in front of them; she noticed him chant something slowly.

You seem very protective of a mundane…" A voice came from behind them, an older woman's voice, strong and shrill like the wave of flowing waters, sharp and piercing. They turned around swiftly almost in unison, Theo subconsciously holding Kallie protectively, using his body as a shield.

"A child of the night and a……. A mundane." She finished her sentence looking slightly puzzled, staring at her long nails the entire time; she flicked her eyes up at them for a moment before she turned around and walked off.

Kallie and Theo looked at each other, baffled, before scampering after her, and right where they had just walked was a cottage. Kallie could have sworn there was nothing there just minutes ago, but she said nothing. Something about this woman made her hold her tongue.

They entered through a strong wooden door, hoping this wasn't a trap.

"We are looking for Morgana." Theo demanded his tone firm and powerful, like the first time he met Kallie in her office.

"You're in luck." She replied with a smirk, "But why do you seek me, *night child?*"

She sat down grinning over a large platter of fruits, only then did they get a good look at her. She was a pretty woman. Kallie thought to herself. Morgana looked to be in her mid-fifties, her skin glowing with life and wisdom, her grey hair wild and frizzy but in an exotic way. She looked like a woman with loads of class, style and taste, maybe a little too much, but she managed herself just fine. She turned her eyes to Kallie, staring right past her body into her soul. Kallie felt naked under her gaze, she looked like she was pleased to see her, or not… she was not so sure,

Kallie let her eyes wander around what seemed like Morgana's living room, which looked more like a showroom for a sorceress, or seer. There was an old mahogany table with Trappola and tarot cards and a big glass full of what looked like smoke in the middle of the room. She stared at the glass trying to figure out how the smoke didn't just disappear out the top; she pushed the thought away her eyes dancing around the room at all the treasures to be seen. It was a sight to behold.

"They tell the future, and the past, would you like a reading?" she asked, gliding past her fruit platter to sit in front of the table. She sat elegantly, her back straight and high like an old British woman with poise and grace. She waved her right hand lightly, almost boneless-looking, and her fruit platter reappeared on the table. She snapped her fingers, and two seats appeared directly opposite her, along with two glasses of wine in tall elegant glasses.

"Sit, have a drink." Morgana waved at the spread in front of her. "Am I really so charming you are both lost for words…?" she continued, looking like she enjoyed the sound of her own voice. "Impressive, I know. Stare away." she tittered.

Theo grabbed the chair closest to him, taking a seat. He had been taking his time, thinking of ways to get the best out of Morgana—witches and warlocks were a very greedy species, they always asked for something priceless in exchange for their services, and for some reason she seemed more interested in Kallie than himself, he was curious too, as was Kallie, so he just let things flow.

"Was that a portal?" Theo asked.

"Yes, leads you right to the Faery Kingdom – to home." At the end of her last two words her eyes flicked to Kallie smirking, she looked like she wanted to say even more but didn't. Kallie frowned confused.

"You have questions, so many of them. Pick a card." She continued, her eyes still trapped in a gaze with Kallie's. Kallie didn't know how she felt about having her fortune read to her, she didn't even pay much attention to zodiac signs in the regular world, but this woman looked like the real deal, and she sure had questions, she has had questions her whole life. She was finally staring at the woman that might be able give her those answers and that terrified her.

She closed her eyes, and drew a card out of the pile, placed it on the table to reveal The Moon card. Morgana took the remaining cards, shuffling mindlessly like she was in a trance, the cards dancing in her fingers, and she hummed to a tune while she felt the cards, and stopped.

"A rare one you are. A child of light." She paused, "Do you know what your name means, child?"

"No… my mother passed when I was young." Kallie mumbled.

"It means *From the Forest*. Like all Fae you have ties here and will always be pulled here."

"Fae…?" Kallie asked puzzled, she glanced at Theo his eyes met hers wide. Morgana continued. "Your mother was pure of heart. She loved everyone; always saw the good in people."

"This has Faerie protection, it belonged to your mother and she gave you her protection." She pointed at the necklace hanging around Kallie's neck, one she had worn her entire life, her dad had made sure she never took it off, made sure she never went a day without it, but she had never thought much of it. She ran her hands over it now, acknowledging the rowan wood inside the pendant—the wood holding a gem stone that she could never identify.

"You knew her…? Where is she?" she asked wide eyed, as thoughts of her mother came to her mind again, this time more alive than she ever imagined.

"That necklace, my dear, led you right to that portal, you are the reason why the portal was visible to you both; it is why the woods welcome you with such open arms." She continued her arms wide, almost out of pity.

"So wait… You're saying I'm a… a Faerie? Are you a Faerie?"

"Of course…" Theo's silence ended as his mind put the pieces together. "This is why my powers don't work on Kallie."

Morgana sneered lightly at him "Well done, you're not just a pretty face then."

She turned back to Kallie, "The Queen of Fae and I, had a long pact, for centuries; she has offered me her protection in exchange for a service. I am a witch. No Fae in my bloodline." She took a bit of a strawberry in her hand, and ran her tongue along the top of her upper lip.

"If you ever want to find out more about your roots, just step into that portal."

Kallie's mind was reeling, "don't Faeries have powers? Why don't I have any?"

"Your mother, oh bless her soul, had so many enemies; she thought living away from this world was the safest for you. After you were born, she brought you here, to hide you away from the kingdom. I created the potion she used on you, it was a rare one, had very dangerous procedures and effects on your mother."

"Is that what happened to her…?"

"As far as I know, she died defending the Kingdom. That is all the rumours that I hear this side of the portal."

Kallie's eyes began to blur as tears formed, a single drop running down her cheek, thoughts of her mother overwhelming her. She brushed the tear away. She didn't want to think about this now, they were here for Theo.

She drove the conversation back to the reason for their visit. "I want to know about a ritual, what we really came here for. One that can turn a vampire back into a human."

"You are just like her, fearlessness in her eyes, wanting to rewrite destiny, seeing only the good in others…" With that last statement she turned her gaze to Theo, Her eyes piercing deep into his, she sighed.

"What you seek is possible, but it comes at a price, like all magic should."

"What do you mean?" He questioned. His chin firm and hard, his eyes filled with worry.

"The spell you seek is the rarest of the night children; its rarity is mostly because of the sacrifice needed for its completion. It requires a sacrifice, a soul."

"So someone has to die for Theo to become human again…?" Kallie queried, her voice wavering. "Not just someone, it requires a vampire soul."

"I want this, but, how can I ask someone to give their soul to set mine free?"

"It is the laws of the universe, to create a balance; an exchange has to be paid."

Kallie's eyes met Theo's, the amber in them less intense as his brow furrowed with worry.

Theo didn't say anything else, his mind raged with endless thoughts. It was possible but it may as well not be. A soul? The universe was a cruel mistress. Finding out that Kallie is a Faerie was one thing to think about, but a willing vampire soul in exchange for his was the least he had expected of this spell.

When they had left home that day he had felt hope anew, like he had never felt before, this life he didn't choose, all he ever wanted was to be normal again. And now it seemed his hopes had been quashed, there's no way they would be able to do this.

"Suflet schimb" Morgana chanted the words, her voice cutting through Theo's thoughts. At that moment another woman walked in, she looked just like Morgana, she said nothing, she walked close to Kallie, regarded her intensely and left almost immediately, Morgana followed.

The door after Morgana's belonged to the other witch, it had words etched at the door post, just like Morgana's. Theo was so lost in his own thoughts he didn't pay attention, but Kallie remembered the words Morgana had just spoken before the silent witch had walked in on them. She saw the words on the wall, but they weren't alone.

"SCHIMB DE SUFLETE; Pentru a ierta viata ai nevoie de un suflet dornic..." She pulled out her phone from her tiny bag just long enough to take a picture of the writing on the wall, she didn't know what language it was, or what these words meant, but she was going to find out.

She hurried to catch up with Theo, as they walked back to the car.

* * *

The ride back to Theo's apartment was quiet; they both had so much on their mind. Different emotions running through them, but one thing was constant, they had so much hope and excitement in their quest to meet Morgana that the reality of the sacrifice for the spell was the biggest setback they had ever imagined. Kallie felt a relief, she didn't want him to go through with this, and she felt a pang of guilt for feeling relieved when he felt this way. She had never seen Theo this cold before, he drove so fast, his hands clenching so hard on the steering wheel she thought it might break, but she said nothing, maybe he would feel better if he let it all out in his driving.

When they arrived neither Theo nor Kallie said a word to each other, she wanted to reach out to him, to touch him, to say something to make him feel better, but she couldn't find the words. She brushed her fingers against his arm lightly as his hands still gripped the steering wheel. She leaned towards him; her lips so close to his she could feel his breathe on her skin. He didn't move, he had never felt so out of control around her before, he had never felt so out of control in decades, his senses were more alert to her pulse, he could smell her blood, he could see her veins pulsing delightfully under her skin. It drove him wild, in ways unimaginable, in ways that scared him, in ways he imagined would scare her away from him.

"Let me take you home." The words rolled out of his tongue before he could as much as hold them back, but even he knew it was for the best. Although they had been together for over a month, she had never seen the monster in him, the monster he always held back, the monster he never wanted her to see. She didn't move, if she was hurt or scared by his attitude, she did a perfect job hiding her emotions behind the insipid look on her face.

"No, I want to be here, with you, I'm sorry about…."

"Don't be, don't be sorry for anything. I just feel… different. I don't think it is safe for you to be here tonight, Kallie."

She reached out to him, like a mother reaching out to her broken child, her hands cupping his face tenderly; she was so sweet he thought, so fragile, so tender.

"I don't want you to hold anything back; I want you to be yourself, your true self, with me."

She kissed him ardently, her tongue ravishing his, parting his unwilling lips, driving her way into not just his lips, but his mind, his very existence. He felt his insides grow still; he didn't want to make love to her like this; he didn't want to see her hurt. But today he didn't have any control over his emotions, and having her kiss him like this, with her hands running wild against his hair, his neck, he didn't think, he just acted.

He carried her out of the car, into his house, and then to the kitchen. She lay over his shoulders like a child helpless, at his mercy.

He positioned her over the breakfast bar, her breasts touching the cool marble making her nipples taut, her hands grasping the bench top. He tucked the hem of her dress to her waist, exposing her round firm butt and the lacy briefs she wore this morning. He ran his hands over it lightly. Kallie's body tingled at his touch. She didn't know what he had in mind, but she was willing to find out. Theo returned with a belt in hand, his shirt unbuttoned to expose his hard torso. He looked like a man who spent his entire life working his body into perfection.

She shivered at the thought of what he might do, she always thought he was being too careful with her when they had sex in the past, she had watched him hold back, but now, she saw a man that did just what he wanted with her body, and the mere thought of this made her drip. She felt the moistness from her own body trickle down her thighs, just like in her dreams before.

He wrapped the belt around her wrists, a light tug and click to tighten making Kallie gasp in pleasure. She tried to move, but every move made the thick leather belt eat more into her skin, the pain it brought excited her more than she imagined.

He was so close to her now, his hard crotch pressing against her rear; she paid attention to all the details, because today, all she wanted to do was to feel. And feel she did. His touch was electric, stroking her hips, her ass, sending signals to her head, and between her thighs. She felt the wetness soaking her thighs greasing the table, just like he had read her thoughts; he reached for her panties, slipping them down and off, falling to the floor soaking wet. One hand gripped her belted wrists, the other pulling on her hips and his thrust was the next thing she felt, hard, his every push drove her to spasms, she cried out in pleasure as he plunged deeper into her, his hand left her wrists as he groaned, he leaned forward his mouth at her ear, his hands grabbing her hair in a delicious pull, his other hand held onto her waist for balance.

She felt her insides clench together as he pushed her to climax, she was moaning so loud she thought someone might call the police. But she didn't care. This was like nothing she had ever felt before, the delicious pain from the belt as it dug into her skin, her slick breasts pressed against the counter. Her body rocked fiercely, his hands changing from her neck to her hair and back again, pulling so hard she could only gasp for air, her body running on overdrive, he didn't stop. She came twice but he didn't stop. Kallie felt his fangs graze her neck, her shoulder, his hand around her neck guiding her. Just lightly and then a little harder, then a little deeper, and deeper until she could feel him suck deliciously, her mind fuzzy but euphoric, the pain on her skin lingering, his hunger, his passion, her excitement, all she could do was feel. He thrust harder, feeding on her rhythmically as her body was awash with waves upon waves of desire, her blood and sweat mixing together before they both collapsed in orgasm together.

CHAPTER TEN

"Are you going to tell me everything now?"

Hana's welcome was stern, her hands on her hips, as soon as Kallie stepped through the front door. She had half expected to be alone, at least that's the way it was normally—Hana was generally out most days—being the social butterfly she was, and it was only 2pm. *Damn, I could really use a nap after last night...* She thought smiling as her memories jumped into last night.

"Hi, Hana, nice to see you too. I'm doing well thanks for asking." Kallie retorted sardonically, "Let me breathe for a second would you, I've just walked in the door". Kallie sighed; she was too tired for a fight; it had been a big couple of days. She sat down, regarding their home slowly. It had only been a few weeks, but everything felt alien and new to her, especially because Hana wasn't exactly the tidiest roommate in the world. Everything looked just a bit out of place. Kallie turned around just enough to expose the bite marks on her neck; she had been so conscious about it, so she deliberately threw a scarf over her neck to cover up and avoid answering questions.

"Girl, are those hickeys I see!? No, I am done letting you breathe, all I have done for the past few weeks was let you breathe and you went MIA on me! Do you realize how worried I have been?" Hana tried to reach for the scarf but Kallie shifted uncomfortably, Hana didn't understand her BFF's new attitude, but she was sure going to get everything out of her this time. She was done with secrets.

"Ha! Look at you sounding like my long lost mother." Kallie stood, swinging her scarf back around her neck before walking fast-paced back to her room, half expecting Hana to follow. She wasn't disappointed, and although she didn't show it, she was glad. She wanted to tell her everything too, she didn't even know how to keep anything from her best friend, she just wasn't sure if Hana was even remotely ready to digest the information she had to share.

How do you tell your perfectly normal best friend that your entirely normal life has been a lie, that you weren't even a regular human being, and oh, the juiciest part: that you have been sleeping with a vampire who fed off you during one of your raunchy love sessions, and oh that you totally loved it too?! She almost snorted out loud playing that thought out in her head.

She sat on her bed pulling her scarf off, and Hana sat right opposite her. One thing is certain—she knew her best friend wouldn't back down until she knew everything she wanted to know; she was going to get the truth out of her one way or another.

"Well, you already know me—if the shoe fits, I'm damn well taking the role. Someone has to."

Kallie didn't react, choosing to pick her battles, "Great, well you already know I've been with Theo..."

"Scratch that, get to the juicy part, you know… the whole he's a vampire thing and when you started forgetting you had a home, and a job. Have you been turning up for work, please tell me that you've been going to work this entire time…'?'" *As expected, impatient Hana wouldn't let me start easy, she really has no idea what is coming.*

"Sort of…Just calm down, okay. Look if you're going to keep talking, I might as well just sit here."

"Okay, fine. You're such a bore. You win, my lips are sealed, ears open, now shoot." She made the lock and key gesture with her hand and lips, throwing the imaginary key across the room.

"These are obviously from him, not exactly easy to hide…" Kallie blushed, waving her hand absently at her neck. Hana leaned closer to inspect the bite wounds.

"He *bit* you? Does that mean you're like…a full blown vampire now? Do I need to kick some serious vampire butt?!" announced Hana, showing off her karate arm movements. "No but seriously, are you ok?"

"I'm fine, Han. No, that's not how turning works apparently. I've been…amazing" Kallie blushed scarlet, once more explaining how the punctures managed to happen and all the inner details of Theo's life.

"Umm… who are you and what have you done with my sweet, innocent Kallie?" Hana retorted, truly shocked, slapping Kallie light heartedly on the thigh.

"I know; I know it's a lot to take in. I'm sorry I haven't been truly honest with you. A lot of shit went down when we found out…" Kallie stopped mid-sentence while Hana's eyes squinted at her in confusion.

"First you have to promise not to freak out; and you can't tell anyone about this, okay? I'm serious, Hana Banana." The carefree vibe in the room suddenly became very sombre as Kallie reached across and grabbed her hands.

"Seriously? You know I'm a woman of my word!" Hana hit her with a pillow. "Cross my heart," she said, making the hand movement over her purple crop top. The look on her face was priceless, like she had just been challenged with some kind of intrepid battle, one she looked ready to win. If there was anything Hana hated, it was being underestimated.

"I know I'm just saying… anyway, I did mention Theo wasn't so normal already, right? Turns out he isn't, at all. Which you now know: Vampire and all that."

"Okay, can I throw in a 'yeah' every so often? Just to let you know I'm following." Hana wiggled her eyebrows, nodding.

"Yeah, just listen, this gets pretty serious from here. We have lot of info to get through.

"Ok so we found a witch, well we tracked down a witch, a real one, and had my cards read." Kallie was rambling, looking at her knotted fingers on her lap. "She knew my mother Han, and my mother… my mother wasn't human."

What the hell did she mean by not human? What…?! She was rambling in her head, completely overrun with thoughts, but she kept her mouth shut. At this point she needed to make it clear she was capable not only of keeping her mouth shut, but of not freaking out. Hana had a wild imagination, and thanks to that she was almost ready for anything. *I mean she got over the vampire thing fairly quickly, didn't she?*

"My mother was Fae, a faery, who got involved with a human; my father, who then birthed me. I'm some sort of half human, half faery hybrid… and that explains why she had to disappear after my birth. It wasn't permitted."

"So… You're a *faery*… and Theo, he is a *vampire*…" Kallie could see Hana's brain working on overdrive behind her eyes.

Hana nodded her head slightly, grinning ear to ear the entire time, not because she didn't have anything to say, but because she couldn't help it—she had a terrible habit of smiling and laughing at the oddest times: when she was angry, shocked, surprised and lately when she gets told by her best friend, the book-loving Kallie, whom she had known since forever, is now a faery with a vampire boyfriend. A faery and a vampire. She was sure she looked crazy right now, but at this moment, crazy was just what she felt.

"This is real Hana, the reason he came to me in the first place was because he doesn't want to be a vampire anymore, and he doesn't want to live this life anymore."

"Well technically he isn't living any life, aren't vampires supposed to be lifeless, soulless bodies?" Hana found her voice again; Kallie looked relieved that she was finally talking.

"It's really different from what we see in the movies, babe."

"But is it though..? Didn't you just up and fall in love with a vampire? Like all the other human girls in movies?" she snorted.

"Right, ok maybe just that bit." Kallie laughed lightly "But this isn't a movie, Theo is alive, and he's an important part of my life now, and I plan to leave it that way. I plan to do all I can to help him with this, even if I love him as he is." This was real. This was happening and she knew already what she would do, whose side she was on.

"So… no sparkles?" Hana tried to lighten the mood again which garnered a swift shoulder hit with a pillow from Kallie. They both laughed.

"You know I'm always here for you. It doesn't matter how stupid your decisions are, which are really stupid if I may add, but I would rather hold your hand and walk that stupid path with you, any day, any time."

"Thank you, Hana; this is why you are the best thing to ever happen to me."

Kallie reached for Hana, she hugged her tight, squeezing her; she felt so much lighter now. Having Hana to talk to, who listens, understands, and accepts her had to be the best gift, a gift she had come to treasure today more than before.

"I know, I know, now stop squeezing me. And tell me everything I need to know. This just got really interesting, like conspiracy theory interesting." Hana wriggled herself free, grinning. She knew the last thing Kallie needed right now was a breakdown.

"How are you not freaked out?"

"Freaked out is what I have been, putting up with your boring ass for so long. Now this, this right here sounds like living. So, tell me, is there any way to make his dream come true? To make him human again?" Hana asked rather seriously; she was so interested in this now more than ever, for some reason she already felt like a huge part of this mission.

"The witch we saw, Morgana, she said there was a spell, but he needs another vampire to give his soul in exchange to redeem his."

"Oh…did he mention how he became one?"

"Yeah, it's really horrible, Han. His uncle was turned many years ago, he was out of control. When you're freshly turned it's so hard to control yourself. He ripped and fed on Theo's entire family, only Theo made it." Kallie explained softly, this part always got to her. "William, his uncle, vanished after that. No one's seen him since."

"Wow, oh my god that's horrible. I want you to know, if there is anything I can do to help you guys I'm all in." Hana declared, seriousness lining her face.

"Theo wouldn't like that, he wouldn't even approve of me telling you honestly, he thinks it's too dangerous."

"Fuck that. I'm your family and that makes him my family too. It might take some time, but he has to learn to accept this. And hey, no more secrets, I want you to promise me this, okay?"

"I promise, you are my breath of fresh air, I feel like a weight has just been lifted off my shoulders." She really meant that, she hoped Hana would understand how important this meant to her.

"Enough about Theo; tell me more about your Mom." She noticed Kallie go gloomy whenever the topic shifted to Theo, she had a feeling it was a result of the witch's visit. She hated to imagine how Theo felt about that, about all of this. He seemed like a nice guy, one her best friend had truly come to love.

"There still isn't much to tell, I still know so little. I do know that she was an incredible warrior and that she died fighting in a great faery war. Also she had a spell cast upon on me at birth, so I would be safe. She had a lot of enemies"

The door-bell rang and Hana ran off immediately, she had ordered a large box of pizza, and was low-key glad he didn't come in few minutes earlier, that would have been the world's worst timed pizza delivery ever.

"Who's that?" Kallie asked from her bedroom, half expecting her best friend to come back telling her she'd invited a man over.

"Pizzaaaaaaa!" Hana walked in with a large box of pizza, the smell wafting through the room. Kallie suddenly remembered how hungry she'd been.

"I'm starved. This time you do the talking, tell me what's been up with you."

CHAPTER ELEVEN

Pulling up at Theo's apartment, Kallie couldn't help but think of a hundred reasons why this was a bad idea, not that the idea of introducing Hana to Theo was terrible in itself, but she knew Theo wouldn't like any of this. He tried to have as little contact with other humans as possible, and when he did, he usually just erased their memories after, just as he almost did with her.

But this was important to Kallie. If Theo needed her to accept him for whom he was and all his baggage then he needed to accept her life as well, and that included her crazy baggage, which of course included Hana. They came as a pair.

Kallie tapped her fingers on her steering wheel anxiously as she turned to look at Hana. She'd spent the entire ride chatting about how she couldn't wait to meet Theo, and what she imagined he looked like, although Kallie made the conscious effort to nod often, and throw in a yes or no accompanied by some small talk. She hardly heard a word, and it was pretty obvious how worried she was.

"If this is a bad time we can always reschedule, babe." She hated seeing Kallie worried and if her meeting Theo was bothering her this much, she could stand to wait a while. Although parts of her needed to know Theo not only because she had decided to help them, but because she had to make sure she was safe. Kallie was family to her, she couldn't think of anything else in the world that would ever console her if anything happened to her best friend.

Kallie stopped tapping, breathing out an exasperated sigh.

"Maybe you want to give it time, let him know you want him to meet me first maybe..." *Sounded like a more reasonable plan.* Hana thought, but Kallie's voice dragged her out of her own thoughts.

"Nope. Let's do this now, before I lose my nerve. Get it done. Plus, he'll know we're here already."

"Not creepy at all..."

"You don't know the half of it." Kallie smirked back.

They got out of the car, hands locked together, both battling a mix of emotions as they walked towards the door.

"Just curious, can one cheat on a vampire? Would he just tell if you went on and…?" Hana tilted her head towards Kallie's shoulder suggestively, using her go-to naughty expression, grinning from ear to ear, both brows raised in slow dance, one lifting after the other.

"Are you ever going to act serious? For once? I'm just curious." Kallie quipped back lightly at her. The elevator door dinged, and she pulled Hana through it as she giggled.

"You are such an old bag of bore sometimes." Kallie snorted. She looked around the house, it looked pretty normal to her, normal yet classy and vintage. *Theo sure had taste.* She thought. There wasn't too much furniture, just enough for a man who never entertained visitors and his boring girlfriend. Theo was nowhere in sight.

"Wait here." She pushed Hana into an armchair. "I'll be back in a minute. And no snooping!" And with that Kallie vanished into the hallway just behind Hana's seat waving a finger at her with caution.

She strolled into the hallway half expecting Theo to stop her, and he did. He looked like carved marble; cold and stern.

"What has gotten into you Kallie? You didn't think to inform me first?" His voice was surprisingly calm despite his harsh exterior. *It was hard to catch him without any control of his emotions* she thought to herself. She smiled back, her hands patting his chest lightly.

"It's ok Theo, she's harmless, plus you'll have to meet her eventually!"

"I am a vampire; do you realize how much danger you are putting your best friend in just by bringing her here?" his voice a little bit higher than earlier, but not high enough to reach Hana. She suddenly looked worried, unsure, and anxious, so much that it made her belly churn with worry.

"Oh come on Theo, you never hurt me even when I was just another regular human to you. You're not a monster, you need to stop treating yourself like one and let the world see you how I see you." She hated to see him belittle himself, he had so much control over his reality, and she admired him greatly for it, but it was too sad to watch him doubt his own strengths this way.

They stood there, staring at each other for a while, Kallie broke the silence.

"I'll go make coffee, give you two time to meet." She grinned at him and pranced away to the kitchen, he stood there, feet fixed to the ground.

He knew that she was right; he knew he wasn't a monster, at least not any longer. More importantly he would never be ready. If this is what Kallie needed from him then he would do it, he dragged her into his world. It was the least he could do. He walked into his living room, Hana on the sofa with her back towards him. He watched her for a while longer; her straight black hair had electric blue tips cut in a short bob just below her jawline before she raised a ringed hand to tuck it behind a heavily pierced ear. She had a certain aura, her halo was fierce but that wasn't all. Hana carried an aura that exuded a powerful blend of personalities, he could tell she had a wild heart, a wild sweet heart, one that can set the world on fire, and Kallie's words came back to him. He liked Hana, he was sure he did, without even having to see her face yet she reminded him of his sister. June had that same fierceness he recognized in Hana. A loyal force.

He waved the thoughts of his family off, dragging himself back to reality with the sound of his own voice.

"Nice to finally meet you, Hana." Half expecting her to be startled at the sound of his voice, to his surprise she turned around calmly, composed, wearing a warm smile as she stretched her hand to him.

"Oh Theo, I'm honoured to place a charming face to our prince charming, finally." She teased, holding a hand out. Theo couldn't help his smile broaden, his chiselled chin curved handsomely as he took her hand in return, Hana couldn't help but think that if there were an actual

Greek god out there he would look exactly like Theo, his dark brown hair looked glossy and out of this world. She could see without any doubt what Kallie talked about during their first meetings; staring into his eyes she caught herself trapped in awe of him, she knew it was the vampire charm, she had seen too many movies not to tell.

"You flatter me." His words like warm velvet.

"You leave me no choice, that's your thing after all." Hana's eyes flashed, her realness was piercing. He felt embarrassment wash over him, he had just tried to charm her into liking him, and not only could she tell; she had no qualms speaking it. Once again his mind drifted to June, thoughts of her endearing boldness, her smile and fierceness. And at that minute he knew Hana had become a part of his life. A part of Kallie, that was now a part of him, and more importantly a part of their team.

Although she was just human, she had so much to offer, he was sure.

Kallie came in just in time with a tray and coffee cups; she placed tray on the table, poured out some for Hana and herself, skipping Theo for obvious reasons.

"I see you two are already bonding without me."

"We thought you'd never come, why pause the party?" Hana retorted. Theo couldn't help but laugh hard, it was so cute seeing Hana and Kallie go back and forth with each other. *I could watch them for decades.*

CHAPTER TWELVE

He had been watching Theodore since he arrived in Amherst. He had spent decades following Theodore, but even William, in all his years of preparation for this moment, still found himself unprepared for this moment.

His chin length silver hair was tossed by the wind as he stood in the woods just opposite Theo's apartment. Days had turned to weeks, since he found Theodore again, but every time he stood here watching, waiting for the right moment to talk with his nephew, it never came. Theo's family had died by his hands, by his fangs, every one of them, what could he have to say to make him feel better? Would there ever be a time good enough to say sorry? Too many thoughts flowed though him, and for the first time in nearly two hundred years he was afraid, and yet he found himself walking towards the front door.

He hit the doorbell quickly, twice, and then decided against it. He turned to walk away until a girl rounded the corner. She was human, he could tell, but she was different. She smiled warmly, her green eyes lighting up, her long blonde hair framing her face and shoulders.

* * *

"Hello… Are you looking for Theo?" She asked confused.

"Hello, ah yes I am here to see Theodore." His voice was husk with age, and class. His preference to calling him Theodore, made her feel at ease—there was a certain familiarity about this man, not only did the name Theodore fondly roll off his tongue, he seemed like a gentleman to Kallie. He wore a three-piece suit, grey tweed with a dusty green scarf.

"Oh sure, come in." She stepped inside the elevator with him when it hit her; she hadn't even asked what his name was.

"I'm Sorry, I didn't catch your name…" She turned around mind question as the doors dinged open, but Theo's voice found her before the man's response. He stood directly in front of the doors, he knew they were coming.

"What are you doing here?" His speed, the tone of his voice—she had never heard him talk to anyone in this manner. In a split second he was standing between her and the silver haired older man, shifting her inside the room.

She needed no one to tell her to excuse them, whatever was going on right now between these two she could tell they needed their privacy, and quite honestly she was slightly terrified to see Theo this angry. He wouldn't be mad at her for letting the man in, whoever he was; Theo was more than displeased to see him.

She left for the bedroom, curiosity ravaging her mind as she shut the door behind her.

* * *

"Theodore, I am sorry to intrude, if you would just give me a minute, just listen, please." Uncle William finally found his voice again.

"Damn right you are sorry. Now get out, I never want to see you again." Theo spoke again, his voice half yelling. Theo was enraged, how dare he just turn up to his house like this. Kallie… He had put her in danger too. Just looking at William brought back memories, memories Theo had kept locked away deep down, memories that had caused him nightmares. All these decades and just looking at him again brought them flooding back in like a tidal wave.

"It's been so very long, every passing year has been just as hard for me as it has for you."

"Just as hard!? Hard FOR YOU?" Theo was yelling now, he couldn't keep his anger in check any longer. "All these years and you show up now to tell me this?" He couldn't believe his eyes, worse he couldn't believe his own ears. *William was here to play the victim?*

"I am so sorry about what happened, and I accept full responsibility, for everything, for you Theodore." William continued the sound of his voice, his very presence drove Theo even crazier, but nothing riled him more than the familiarity with which his name rolled off of his tongue.

"Don't you dare call me that!" He yelled back, his own fury surprised him, he flung his arm against Uncle William in a hard blow, but instead he hit the wall hard, so hard he saw the crack on the wall after him—an evidence of his own rage. He couldn't remember the last time he was this furious, at anything, at anyone.

"Get out. Now. You are not welcome here." He was at the door again, gesturing for William to leave, his nostrils flared, amber eyes blazing.

"I cannot stay away from you Theodore, you know this, surely all these decades you must have learnt this. Please."

"Leave, before I do something I end up regretting."

* * *

William turned around; he didn't expect to be welcomed by his once favorite nephew with a smile, but he had expected a bit more than this. It had been over 120 years since that incident. He thought enough time had passed. A man could only apologize when listened to; he wished Theodore would give him time. He didn't mean to hurt him, to hurt any of them, but surely even Theo knew about how blood thirsty new vampires become. If he had any control at all this wouldn't have happened, but even William knew these were just excuses.

* * *

Theo was fuming, he stood there minutes after Williams exit gathering his thoughts, shallowing his breathing. He never imagined William would show his face again. During his first few decades as a vampire he played around with what he would do to him if they ever crossed paths again, the ideas tortuous and arguably cruel. But now out of the blue, when he had least expected it, he didn't know how to react. This man shows up trying to give an apology, for doing this to him. *Would anything he had to say ever make him feel forgiveness?* Theo doubted it. He heard Kallie walk up behind him.

"Are you ok…?" She wrapped her arms around his torso, resting her cheek against his shoulder blade. Theo's breathing slowed, calmness seeping over him as he felt her warmth, but he didn't answer.

"Who was that?" Kallie tried again, lightly.

"That was my Uncle William, I told you about him… about the…"

"I remember," Kallie cut him short, not wanting him to relive any further bad memories. "I'm sorry for letting him in, I assumed he was a friend, it's for the best anyway; that you made him leave. For all of our safety. You did the right thing. " She couldn't stop talking, she just wanted to say something, anything to make him feel better, to make him stop staring into space like he was right now. Like a man caught in a trance, but she couldn't find the words. Not the right ones, anyway.

* * *

The next few hours, she watched Theo try to act like he was okay, like he wasn't hurting, although she acknowledged his efforts to feel good for her sake; she wished that he would trust her enough to let his emotions show in front of her, to share all of his pain. That night when they made love, it was intense, raw. His hurt showing as their emotions entwined together like vines wrapping a tree.

He kissed her slowly, his lips digging into hers with unmatched hunger, she didn't try to match her hunger with his, she just felt the pleasure his tongue created. Her legs shivered as his lips trailed down her body, kissing, pinching, grabbing and nibbling on every inch he came in contact with, leaving a wake of goose bumps. She quivered, her back forming an arch as his lips travelled down her waistline, her hands reached for his hair, pushing his head deeper between her thighs, but he caught her wrists together, holding them prisoner just above her belly button while his teeth and tongue left their trail marks in the most intimate parts of her body.

"Don't move, just ask." He whispered not to her ears, but in between her thighs, kissing and biting, each word dancing a little longer than the one before. She heard his hands unbuckle his belt, her stomach clenched her mind remembering the last time he used it. He bound her wrists together before attaching that to the headboard.

"Please…" She whispered.

He stepped back regarding her body slowly, almost like he was tapping into her every thought, and the thought of his reading her mind at this moment made her feel naughty, like a child caught stealing out of her favorite candy jar. She blushed hard, but unnoticed, because parts of her skin were already red with pain and sweetness. He looked at her like a newly unwrapped gift box, taking in all the details of her body. This woman, whose body led him to do unimaginable things to her.

He moved closer, rubbing his skin deliberately against hers, his right hand grabbed her neck hard, forcing her to tilt for comfort while his lips travelled from her right breast, to the left, suckling delicately and hard at intervals. She tried to move, her hands tugging deliciously against her restraints, his body pressing hard against hers, her neck held onto by his dominant hand, every move she tried to make hurt her deliciously, and every pain she felt was followed by pleasure and excitement. He smelled amazing. All of her senses were on fire. Her bright green eyes met his, her body tingling beneath him with excitement; his lips toured her neck and shoulders while his hard cock pressed for home inside of her. She knew he had been holding out on her before, but this time was different, it was primal. His thrusts were welcomed by her glorious wetness, her gasps and moans played a sweet tune to his ears, her body delicate and slick with sweat fuelling his excitement. Kallie arched further as he delved deeper inside of her, his hand grasping her blonde hair to one side exposing her pale neck. His teeth bit into her skin, first without his fangs, or maybe with them, she couldn't tell, his thrusts were too distracting, his lips too demanding, her body riding into orgasm more intense than she had ever felt before. Her world was a haze, euphoria enveloping her. Kallie could feel him take her to the bathroom and run her a bath, but she just lay there, spent, until the rays of the sun welcomed her eyelids to dawn.

CHAPTER THIRTEEN

"Can we just have one of our classic Friday nights tonight? It's been ages since we really got to have some fun." Hana begged through Kallie's mobile.

"You know, Theo was saying the same thing today, it's just these days partying hasn't really been my top priority."

"There she goes again, grumpy grandma." Hana retorted, "Loosen up; Theo is right, you need to have some fun, come on! Let's meet at Antonio's that pizza place for dinner at six thirty, and we can talk about what to do with the rest of the night!"

Kallie rolled her eyes. *If I had a penny for every time you've called me grumpy, we would be millionaires.* But she knew better than to start that argument with Hana on the phone. Plus it did sound fun.

"Dinner sounds great, I'm starving, been so caught up with work, I totally forgot to eat lunch." She heaved a sigh as the realization of how hungry she really was hit her.

"Awesome, don't be late."

"See you soon."

Kallie dropped the phone and stared frustratingly at her desk. Everything was a mess, from term papers, to her research work, all staring right back at her. She heaved a sigh, running her hands through her hair; ugh it needs a wash, glanced at her desk clock. She had roughly two hours to get all this work done. She knew she needed the entire weekend to sort all this junk out, and be ready for the school conference. But… she knew Hana was right, these past few weeks they've spent so much time apart and they needed to catch up.

Dr. Gale walked in just in time to remind her of the school conference and her presentation as the representative of the department.

More work to remember and sort. An hour later Kallie had her conference speech down, graded her last paper and packed up the rest of her work to finish over the weekend.

* * *

Kallie and Hana walked into Antonio's, neither of them aware of the man following them closely, the hustle and bustle of the restaurant creating a distraction. William had been tailing Kallie for two days now, he waited for a time when he thought it would be best to approach her, and when he watched her drive to the restaurant, he knew this was his only moment. She wouldn't make a scene in public, and he needed her as calm as possible.

They settled into their seats at the far end, which was their favorite, far from the ears of other customers but with a stunning view outside. A blond waitress came in to get their orders and returned with two servings pepperoni pizza and two glasses of wine; they had barely finished their meal when William walked to their table.

"Hello, Kallie."

William was dressed to the nines in a classic tailored blue suit, looking extremely overdressed for the occasion just like their last meeting; he grabbed the empty seat next to them, unbuttoning his suit jacket as he sat down lightly.

"What do you want, William?" Kallie retorted with a tough drawl, surprising even herself as her nerves had just spiked. It was probably the wine, she another took a sip in a bid to act as normal as possible, and for more courage.

"I just need to talk with you, I need to talk with Theodore and you are my best bet right now." His voice was as calm, as the day before.

Hana widened her eyes in disbelieve, her eyes flicking from Kallie to the strangely attractive grey haired gentleman in front of her, *was he another vampire?* Kallie was putting on a good front but she could tell she was frightened of this man.

His deep maroon eyes were fixed on Kallie, something about the way this man talked made his words echo in Hana's head like she was in a trance, singing her mind to sleep, yet her body remained wide awake.

"Theo would be so angry if he knew you were here, you have to leave now."

"What's going on here, you heard the lady, please leave or we'll have to get security." Hana found her voice;

even though he looked harmless, Kallie seemed overly troubled and Hana knew now that vampires are never what they appear.

Kallie sighed, her fear subsiding. "It's okay Hana; we don't have to cause a scene. What do you want William?"

"To say that I am sorry," he paused, "that I regret all that has happened and I accept all of the responsibilities."

"Well isn't this apology coming over a century too late?" Kallie snapped back.

"It is never too late to do the right thing."

Kallie's face softened; she knew it couldn't be easy for William living with what he had done to his family, it didn't excuse his actions but she sympathized with him. "You know it makes no difference to Theo, he won't listen."

Williams gaze fell; his face seemed to age a decade as he fiddled with his cufflink.

"I know about your research, and his quest—I have gone to see Morgana myself, she informed me of what needs to be done to redeem Theo's soul." William's heavy eyes finally lifted to look at them both. "I am willing to pay the sacrifice."

Hana's mind began to tick over, if this was about the ritual, about Theo's quest, then this must be Theo's Uncle, the same one responsible for his family's untimely demise. It started to make sense—the way he carried himself, the way he spoke and dressed. *How many more vampires are lurking around in Amherst?*

She flicked her eyes around the room quickly hoping to spot some.

"Have you told Theo this?" Hana spoke, finally understanding enough to join the conversation.

"Sadly, he will not listen; Kallie was a witness to that." He nodded to Kallie, half expecting her to affirm his statement. Kallie's brow furrowed, she understood why Theo was so angry but…

"Well, he has a fucking right to be, Mr!" Hana throwing her words in his face. Kallie nearly giggled at Hana's brashness with a dangerous vampire. She has absolutely no fear.

"He's right though; I've never seen Theo so angry at anyone before, William could hardly get a word in." Kallie replied. Could she trust William? It might be their only shot at helping Theo.

"Why would you do this? You'll die."

"I did this to Theodore. He doesn't deserve to live this monstrous life, and I want to give him mine, so he can have his life back. It is only right"

Kallie's gaze softened again as she heard him speak so dearly of Theo.

"You should talk to him again." Kallie suggested. Hana watched on nodding in agreement.

"I know, Theo. I watched him grow into the man he is, I see how he looks at you, and I know that you can help me talk to him, help me get through to him."

"I could help you convince him, too. I mean, we need all the help we can get." Hana suggested.

"Thank you so much, both of you, you don't know how grateful I am that you would do this." He took their hands lightly, genuine gratefulness filling his eyes. He stood, preparing to leave.

"How can we contact you?" Kallie asked after him.

"I'll find you."

CHAPTER FOURTEEN

Before they got back to Theo's apartment, they both decided they were too spent to plan another outing, Hana found herself a spot in the living room, while Kallie sorted out the bottles of cider Hana had insisted they get on their way back. Theo walked in just moments after them, grabbing Kallie by the waist, swinging her around for a kiss on the lips, then her chin and neck until she wriggled free, blushing. He turned towards the living room, "Hello Hana, I thought I might have scared you off from visiting again", his signature lopsided smile appearing.

"I'm afraid you're not getting rid of me that easy." Hana smirked.

"Rid of you? God no, what would I ever do without you? I'd positively perish without you, oh, Hana." Theo shot back sarcastically

"Ooo it burns!" Hana laughed turning to Kallie, pausing for a split second, "I'll admit, this boy has game!" Kallie and Theo looked at each other and almost as if that was some kind of cue they burst into laughter.

"And that makes me so glad you've finally met your match." Kallie replied in Theo's defence.

"Well, technically he is your match." Hana pointed out.

"I'm still here ladies," He squared his shoulders as though to announce his own presence.

They all grabbed a drink, apple ciders for the girls and blood bags for Theo; Kallie sat on the couch curling up next to Theo with Hana across from them.

"I met William today… we met William today." Kallie stated, nodding towards Hana to discern her as the 'we'. Theo sat up abruptly his arm unwrapping Kallie's shoulder.

"I can't believe him, why is he bothering you? Did he try to do anything?" Theo's nostrils flared as he sat up straighter, more alert to his surroundings, eyes flashing.

"No, no Theo, it's fine, he just wanted to talk. We weren't in any danger." Kallie assured him, looking at Hana for back up.

"Honestly, Theo, we were safe." Hana chimed in.

"William is dangerous, you know this, stay away from him, make sure you're never alone with him, ever." Theo continued, half ignoring her assurances. He knew his uncle too well—he knew William was bad news, and he didn't want him anywhere near Kallie, or anyone he cared about ever again.

"He apologised. About everything. And honestly I believed him, he was sincere." Hana continued, trying to help Kallie out on this derailing train.

"Right." Theo smirked taking a swig from his, thankfully, non-transparent glass.

Hana knew he was being sarcastic, but she sensed this was the chance for them to convince him otherwise, to tell him of William's intentions. "While I don't fully trust him yet, the man I saw today was sincere—plus I'm a good judge of character."

"So were my parents, sometimes the calmness in a man's eyes says nothing of the darkness within."

He started to dive into a lecture when Kallie's voice cut him off. "He was a fresh vamp, Theo! You know how strong the cravings are, how difficult…" Kallie paused "Look. He found out about your quest, I'm not sure how but he knows everything. He knows about my research, and how long and hard you've been searching for this."

"That's why he came looking for Kallie, he said he wanted to help." Hana continued, seizing the opportunity of Theo's loss of speech. She raised her brow, towards Kallie, in search of some kind of unspoken approval from her best friend. Kallie, nodded slightly.

"Oh? And how does he plan to help?" Sarcasm dripping off of each word.

"He wants to give his life in exchange for yours. He wants to be the soul sacrificed in the ritual, Theo." Kallie replied, she grabbed his hands, her eyes sharply meeting his. She hated being harsh but he needed to hear this.

"I don't need any help from him." Theo retorted scowling, just the mere thought of it pissed him off. He wasn't surprised his uncle would try to use Kallie to get to him, he was just as sly, and manipulative as he remembered. *Why did he think showing up after two hundred years with some sick apology and a prank would make it all go away?* He didn't trust his Uncle one bit, for all he cares this could just be a ploy, some game, a plan to hurt Kallie. Even if it wasn't, he didn't want to find out. He didn't have to be at the mercy of the same person who put him here in the first place. There had to be a better option. Theo's face screwed up in frustration knowing, deep down, there was no other option. And time was running short.

As though she had just read through his thoughts Hana responded, "Look at it this way Theo, he's giving you what he owed you all these years—a human life. A life you were robbed of. In the end, you really have nothing to lose, but if you don't, you will always wonder 'what if'."

"He could hurt you, Kallie, or Hana, for that matter. There is everything to lose." He ran a hand along her cheek softly; Kallie leaned into it, placing a hand on top of his.

"It's okay if you don't want him to help, I don't think the ritual is necessary anyway." Kallie appealed when she sensed his refusal, she had tried many times to stop him from pursuing the ritual, and she just didn't trust the process. Something about swapping souls and someone having to be sacrificed seemed a bit too dark for her liking.

"Oh please, don't start." Theo said in exasperation. Kallie was about to go into one of her long debates on why this was such a bad idea, and he didn't want her to, not now, not here.

"What's so exciting about being human anyway? It's so… so normal." Kallie finished.

"You know Kallie is right, what if something goes wrong? What if….."

Theo cut Hana's sentence midway, "Mundanes are always too scared to chase what they want, always wanting to play it safe. What if something goes wrong? What if? What if…"

"We play it safe because mundanes can actually die. You know… death?" Hana retorted, making Theo stop for a moment, mouth slightly open.

"I know it is dangerous. But what if I never find out? I want this, for me. I have to try. I hope you two understand that."

"Then accept his offer!" Kallie and Hana echoed in unison.

"Like I said—you have nothing to lose." Hana continued.

"I will always support whatever you want to do, Theo." Kallie added.

"Okay." He threw his hands in the air mindlessly as if surrendering. They were right he thought. He had nothing to lose. All Hallows Eve was coming up fast and he may not get another shot at this. "I don't trust him, but I'll talk to him."

CHAPTER FIFTEEN

No sign of her for three days. Kallie frantically searched the house for some kind of clue as to where Hana might be. This wasn't normal; it was very unlike Hana to just disappear without letting her know where she was going for days at a time. Especially now, after their plans with Theo. They were only days away from Halloween and they needed to be ready for the ritual. *Where was she...?*

All attempts to reach Hana had been futile. Her calls kept going straight to voicemail, there was no note anywhere in the house to give any information about her possibly travelling anywhere or visiting a new boyfriend, and what scared Kallie most of all was Hana's clothes left untouched at their house. She didn't pack a bag, and that meant only one thing: She didn't mean to stay out this long.

Thoughts on the endless possibilities of where Hana could be at the moment and how much danger she could be in swamped Kallie's mind.

What if something happened to her? What if she was in danger? What if... What if...

She felt a hard lump in her throat, thoughts jumbling her mind. Her eyes welled with tears and immediately she felt the hair on her skin prick upwards.

Something was definitely wrong with Hana. She picked up her phone to dial Theo's number just as he called her.

"What's wrong?" Theo's deep magnetic voice met her ears.

"I… I. She's gone… I ca-can't find her… Please come over! Hana... something has happe-" She stuttered through her sentences, her voice cracking. She knew she wasn't making any sense, but she didn't know how to string the words together, words to express how much danger she felt in her gut that her best friend was in.

"Calm down Kallie, you need to breathe, one sentence at a time. What's wrong with Hana?"

"She ha… hasn't been home in three days." Kallie sniffed, wiping away tears and trying to squeeze her words out, willing her voice to work.

"I'm sure she's probably somewhere having fun. You know Hana, she's pretty impulsive, and she can take care of herself."

"That's why I'm worried, Theo."

Didn't he get it? Hana loved to communicate, it didn't matter what it was about—she was a talker, this has never happened before. "You don't understand, she always calls or messages. She hasn't even posted on any of her social media. Something's wrong."

He took a long pause, as if he was only just starting to see reason with her. "And you've tried calling her?"

"Three days, non-stop. All of her calls keep going straight to voicemail, like her phones off. Her phone is never off. I'm really worried; I have a bad feeling about this." She responded even before the end of his question.

"I'm on my way."

Kallie sighed and dropped her phone on the bed just as she heard the door click open, relief flooded her. "I'll never get used to that super speed." She smirked lightly, but her heart wasn't in it and she was glad he was here.

"You should rest; I'll go out and check around town to see if anyone has seen Hana."

"I want to come with you, I need to." She stood up immediately and started searching around hysterically for a jacket or a change of pants.

"You look terrible Kallie; did you get *any* sleep last night?"

"I did… sort of. It doesn't matter, I can help, and there are a few places I can remember she likes to go, we should check." Kallie insisted her voice shrill yet firm.

"That's fine, but first you need to get a hold of yourself. Go look in the mirror." His hands resting on her shoulders as though she was some defiant teenager he was trying get back in line.

He had never seen her so distressed over anything before, but something kept telling him Hana was just fine. Hana was the type to live in the moment, go home with a guy she'd just met at a bar or travel to Mexico on a whim. He could imagine her somewhere, doing shots, having the time of her life with a new man, and he didn't mean this in a judgemental way, it's just the way Hana was. She was adventurous and a risk taker, in all the ways that Kallie wasn't. The way he saw it, an adult was allowed to have a few days off from the world, but Kallie was working herself up and he'd help her as much as he could.

He regarded her slowly as she made her way to the full length mirror hung on the back of her bedroom door. *Jesus...* Theo was right—she looked a mess, rumpled track pants paired with an old band tee stained from many a midnight feast. *Was she even wearing a bra...?* She rubbed the mascara out from under her eyes, only just now remembering that she forgot to take off her make-up yesterday. It was just three days without her best friend and she could pass for a mother who had just lost a child. Track pants exchanged for jeans and a fresh unstained T-shirt on, she quickly threw her hair into a ponytail before swiping the red hoodie hanging off her bed post.

"Ok, let's go."

Although she had on a fresh change of clothes, she still wore the same worried look on her face as they began driving through the city streets. They first drove to Antonio's, Kallie and Hana's favorite restaurant, but the waiters said they hadn't seen Hana since the last time she had been there with Kallie. Kallie still insisted on talking to all the workers, even carrying a photo of Hana on her mobile to show them and any customers that would listen. Theo lightly pulled her by the arm and suggested that they try other places.

Then they drove over to The Works cafe, then to the other bars in town—the same answers. No one had seen Hana around, and with every new café, bar, and restaurant they visited, with every negative response they got from every person they walked up to, Kallie broke a little more inside. It was late into the night, about 11:30pm when Theo suggested they try out a few night clubs. He insisted Hana would probably be in one of the clubs having the time of her life, but no matter how optimistic he was trying to stay about Hana's disappearance, it didn't seem to make Kallie feel any better.

They arrived at Lit night club at exactly 12:30 am. And although the club had been open since 10:00pm there was still a long line of people outside waiting to get in—teenagers holding hands, dressed to the nines, lovers clinging to each other as though one might float away if they ever let go. Kallie noticed a couple fighting to the side. The woman was yelling and throwing her hands in the air like a deranged juggler, Kallie wondered what he may have done to make her so aggravated in public, but before she could let her thoughts travel any further Theo had already charmed the bouncers and was pulling her inside looking extremely underdressed.

The music was hard and electric, people dancing to the tune, bumping into each other. Theo held her hand like an under-aged teenager visiting a club for the first time, or maybe like he didn't want her to go missing too. They talked with the waiters and bar men, and were close to giving up when one of the ladies at the bar remembered seeing Hana two nights before. She talked about an older-looking man meeting her here and having a few drinks together. Theo made her describe the older man, and with the ladies description, it fit into Uncle William's looks. Theo asked so many questions and although she waved her blonde hair in exasperation at the arrival of each new question, she answered all of them.

When they left the club, Kallie was officially more worried than she had been before; if Hana was last seen with William two days ago, and her phone kept reaching voicemail. Something was definitely wrong. She hated to think of the possibilities of what might happen to Hana, and immediately started to blame herself for telling Hana any if this, for bringing her into this crazy dark world without any form of protection.

Theo said nothing besides assuring Kallie he would get Hana back. Deep down though, Theo was worried. He knew William was dangerous. But he didn't want to worry Kallie anymore than she already was. Theo pulled up to his apartment and turned around to carry Kallie in. That night, she just curled up staring into space, while he talked and talked, trying to make her feel better.

CHAPTER SIXTEEN

Late into the night while Kallie curled up asleep in his arms, Theo felt the presence of someone else, someone strangely familiar. He carefully untangled himself from Kallie while she slept soundly and headed for the front door.

Every step he took drew him closer to this creeping aura, it felt familiar but laced with layers of darkness, but he saw no one walk in. He walked swiftly around the house. It didn't take long before he spotted her lying on the floor—it was Hana, he could recognize her even with his eyes closed, but she had a certain halo around her, something more powerful subdued her original self, he didn't need a witch to confirm that.

He rushed to her side, her clothes worn out, torn and faded, although he was certain she had only worn these for three nights now they looked so washed up even their colors appeared faded—her jacket half torn, the jean pants she wore ripped off from her calf down to her feet, her tank top ripped in half. She lay on the cold tiles like she was in a coma, her hair looked worse: washed up and matted, the blue on the tips nearly completely washed out. He reached out to carry her but she fought him off as soon as he touched her.

It was hard to believe he had spent the past few minutes watching her passed out lifeless in front of him; the strength in her hands as she wrestled him away from her was impressively powerful, too powerful. He was sure now beyond reasonable doubt she was under some kind of dark force. Before he could utter the words, "Calm down Hana, it's just me. It's Theo." She let out a scream, her voice shrill, sharp and soul piercing, her hands pressed to her head so hard, as though releasing the pressure would lead to its explosion, her fingers dug deep into her scalp.

Kallie heard the screams in her sleep, she could've sworn that was Hana's voice, could have sworn it was a dream. Although she stopped hearing the voice now, it didn't stop ringing in her head. She grabbed a blanket off the floor, wrapped it over her slender body and started off to the living room.

"Hana… Hana!" She rushed right past Theo towards her best friend on sight, but she had only gotten close enough to see Hana closely when Theo pulled her back. "Don't touch her, I tried to get her up and she let out that scream, we can't handle another one of those."

"Wait, what is wrong with her? What is wrong with you, Han?" She turned to her best friend, but Hana didn't raise her head, she only continued pulling on her hair like someone suffering from a nervous breakdown. They stood there watching her, after a few seconds she stopped; she raised her head, staring at Kallie, her eyes which once were brown were now pure black enveloping evens the whitest reaches of her eyes. Her lips looked like they'd baked in the sun for a thousand years, and something about the way she looked at Kallie made her skin crawl all over her body. She pulled the blanket tighter around her.

This isn't Hana. There was something cold and dark in her eyes. Something inexplicably powerful and dark.

"She's possessed. By a demon." Theo concluded. Kallie stared hard at him, her eyes filled with questions, and more importantly, fear.

"A demon…?" She muttered to herself. Theo reached out to hug her, her body fitting into his like a key to a lock.

"We need to get her to Morgana." He said. His hands patting on her hair was the most consoling feeling, she sniffed hard on his skin taking in his smell as if it made her reality more bearable.

She clung to him tightly. She didn't know what else to do, how else to act, she didn't know what to say or think, she had no idea how to feel right now, so she let him be her strength. Hana was in danger. She was a shadow of herself, and she felt worse because she didn't know the heights and limits to demon possession, and just thinking of it made her stomach churn.

"Do you think this has anything to do with her meeting your uncle?"

"It could be I told you two William was bad news."

"I should've listened to you."

"It's alright; it's nothing Morgana can't handle."

"Can we reach William? Finding out what happened could help." Kallie suggested, but her thoughts and speech were interrupted by Hana.

She was saying something.

"William will pay for taking my souls. He will pay for taking what is due me."

"Your souls…? What?" Kallie asked impulsively.

"Souls belong in purgatory" She garbled voices of a dozen people spewing from Hana's mouth "MY SOULS!" She snarled.

"It's the demon speaking, it's not Hana." Theo tried to explain.

"But he's saying something right? Something that might answer some of our questions." Kallie insisted, but Hana wasn't answering any of her questions anymore. She started to scream again, holding her head so tight Kallie was scared she would break her own skull.

Theo locked up the doors and beckoned Kallie to join him on the couch. She sat there staring at Hana, watching her closely until Kallie fell asleep again in his arms.

William arrived that morning, Kallie had no idea how he found them but she was glad he did. As soon as he got in Theo started to yell at him, blaming and accusing him for putting Hana in this position. Kallie first heard their voices while she was in the shower, she rushed through it, and hurried out to meet them arguing.

"Stop it you two, you can tear yourselves apart later but we need to get Hana help."

"Let me take her to Morgana, this is all happening because of me. I should be responsible for this." William countered.

"You should have acted more responsibly than bringing a mundane into all this."

Kallie interrupted, "Theo, you need to cool off. No William, we're not leaving Hana under your care, look where that landed us." Kallie finished her sentence, grabbed her bag and headed for Hana to take her to the car.

Theo drove while William sat in front with him, Kallie and Hana in the back. Kallie wanted to reach out to her, to hold her close and tell her everything would be fine, but she couldn't. Hana looked petrified, and any time anyone tried to go close to her she let out high pitched screams and curses at William for stealing souls destined for purgatory. Kallie knew nothing about purgatory or these stolen souls but she knew she needed her best friend back. She worried about the possible effects the demon might be having on Hana's mind—she couldn't bear seeing her like this.

* * *

Morgana led them into a room designed specifically with ancient signs and sigils, no windows only stone walls and ceiling. The halls of the room were higher than the house looked from the outside, it was dark and strange. Kallie shivered, the whole room made her feel uneasy.

She watched Morgana draw a large circle at the center of the room, then an equally large triangle inside the circle. She swirled in the middle of the circle, swinging her body in a wild dance, clapping her hands at intervals. Kallie noticed she had changed her nail polish and hair color since the last time, her nails were a sharp green, matching the color of the eyeliner on her under eye lid. Her hair had matching green strands and her dress was white as snow. The fluidity in the way she moved her body struck Kallie the most. She beckoned them to move closer, and asked that they bring Hana to the middle with her. Theo and William did as she asked. She instructed them to stand on each edge of the triangle, holding hands together forming a triangle with their arms.

"Stay connected whatever happens" Morgana advised.

Kallie held on to Theo's hand on the right and William on the left, Morgana and Hana remained in the middle between them as she begun the ceremony. Morgana raised her voice in a chant, while her body moved fluidly, her hands clapping at intervals; her eyes were wide open, pure white. Kallie grabbed Theo's hand extra tight, looking to him for reassurance but he was too worried about William. Morgana chanted in a language Kallie didn't recognize, and most of the time Kallie kept her eyes shut in her bid to control her fear. Suddenly there was a pressure in the air, like when you fly in an aeroplane, pressing in from all sides. A strong wind began with no windows for it to stem from; Hana screamed clutching at her chest ripping at her clothes. Her mouth opened unnaturally wide towards the ceiling and a thick dark smoke billowed out, filling the space above the circle. Hana slumped to the floor, unconscious.

"Hana!" Kallie yelled wanting to reach towards her. "Don't break the circle!" Morgana shrieked over the clamour.

Suddenly the garbled voices that they'd heard before spoke again but this time is wasn't through Hana it was coming from the smoke; "Why do you disturb my peace?"

"You don't belong here." Morgana yelled in return.

"I do as I please." The voices cackled maniacally. "You can't send me back... and even if you do I'll be back soon enough, to take what is due to me, to take payment for my souls. I will find you, William."

Morgana's dance grew even more violent, she moved her body bonelessly, her voice overpowering. It wasn't long before the roof above them opened, letting out the dark mist from above their heads, and shutting itself up immediately after. Morgana's dance continued but her chants were reduced by the second. Soon no one heard her voice anymore, just her fingers clapping and the sounds of her metallic rings clanging on each other.

Their hands dropped and Kallie rushed to Hana immediately. "Han...? Please. Hana...?"

Please be okay.

* * *

They left Morgana's cottage very late that night, Kallie in the back seat cradling Hana like a baby while she still slept. Theo and William were silent, the tension was thick.

"I'm sorry…" William began. Theo's lips pursed; "I knew your being here would cause trouble. You put Hana in danger, Kallie also."

"I didn't realize I was being followed. I only wanted to talk to Hana I swear it."

Theo's voice was low but heated. They continued to argue for most of the journey and Kallie didn't intervene. They needed to work through things and what better way than to be in a locked car, not that that would stop a vampire from leaving.

"I want to do this for you, Theo. I regret what I did to you…to our family." William paused, "Let me repay you one last favour and you will never have to see me again."

Theo's standpoint softened as his old Uncle began to surface again.

"I can never forgive you for what you did…" Theo began, "But I can see you feel guilt for what you caused me."

"I accept your offer."

William nodded understanding his eyes closing lightly.

CHAPTER SEVENTEEN

Theo and Kallie sat on either side of Hana's bed, watching her intensely as they had for the past forty eight hours since their return from Morgana's. She had neither stirred her body nor opened her eyes. Morgana had told them it was normal and that she needed all the rest her body could manage, but it scared Kallie to watch her sleep lifelessly like she was in a coma.

"Let's make some coffee." Theo said, cutting into her thoughts.

"Can we call Morgana? Maybe this rest is taking too long." Kallie suggested, half ignoring his suggestion for coffee, her eyes fixed on Hana's pale body, sweeping her hair out of her face. They had sponge bathed her and tried to fix her hair as best they could.

"If she isn't up before nightfall we will make the call." He led her to the kitchen, put the coffee maker on and sat opposite her. His eyes feasted not only on the beauty her body adorned itself with but on how beautiful her soul was, how large her heart was. These past few days he had seen a different side to Kallie, and he loved her even more.

"I love you." The words played out of his lips like a tune to her ears—she loved this man, she loved his voice, the pale shade of his skin which was her new favorite color. She loved how he loved her, and she knew she couldn't say this enough, because she could not find the words to qualify how much she did.

"I love you too, Theo." She smiled at him for the first time in a few days.

He leaned forward pressing his lips to her forehead, Hana sighed. He pulled in her for a full kiss, his mouth gently caressing hers.

"Get a room already." Hana shot lazily at them as she walked into the kitchen. They turned around abruptly, both wearing long-stressed and worried expressions. Kallie rushed to Hana's side, holding her gently.

"Okay, isn't it too early to get all sweet on me? I literally just woke up."

"Oh, shut up. I've been worried sick about you, sit right here. Are you okay? How do you feel?" Kallie led Hana to a sit on the couch and poured her a cup of coffee.

"Well my body feels like I got hit by a truck, my head aches like a bitch, no, I am not hung over, I don't remember drinking last night." She paused to think, "I don't remember anything from last night." She continued.

"You don't remember…anything?" Theo asked.

"Strangely, nothing at all." She replied rather innocently, "And I'm not usually a blackout drinker!" She finished laughing sipping her coffee. Kallie and Theo flashed each other knowing looks. *How could she not remember anything at all?* Kallie thought to herself, *Morgana didn't mention anything about this.* She started to panic again.

"What was the last thing you remember doing?" Theo asked again.

"I remember going out for a few drinks." She paused to think for what seemed like a split second and then continued, "I also remember meeting with your Uncle at the club." She said, pointing at Theo and continued, "I remember walking to my car last night, but I don't remember driving home, which is strange because I wasn't even drunk or anything. I had like two drinks max." This time she turned to Kallie, her brows twisting up in a frown.

Kallie was relieved. She heaved a deep sigh and wriggled her shoulders in a mild shrug, it was a relief to know that this whole experience had not affected Hana's mind, and having Hana talk about not remembering anything had only driven her fears on overdrive. But surely if Hana remembered going out up until she was possessed by that demon then she was relieved.

"Okay..." Kallie said, pausing to take a sip of her own coffee, "First off, that didn't happen *last* night, that was *five* nights ago—you went missing on Friday and appeared three days after looking as rough and sick and disturbed as anyone can imagine. We were so worried; we looked all over town for you!" She paused again, giving Hana time to digest all of this. Hana stared at Kallie jaw-dropped. It was hard to think anyone would be oblivious of their activities for over five days, and even harder was accepting you are that person. She swallowed hard, pushing past the hard lump that had formed in her throat. It was like something out of a movie script, only this time she was in the lead role, she started to think hard about the drinks she had last night… wait no, five days ago. Ok she's never been that drunk before.

"What was I doing for three whole days?" Hana asked confused.

Kallie looked at Hana's worried face; "We don't know, Han. But when you came back you were…possessed."

"Fucking possessed?! Like the exorcist possessed?" Hana blurted wildly.

"Well not exactly…" Theo answered, shrugging lightly.

"We took you to Morgana, she saved you. She performed some ritual, casting out the demon who took control of you, and you have spent the past two days in bed sleeping. We were just considering calling Morgana again." Kallie rushed through the gory details of the entire experience and William's role while Hana listened wide eyed.

"Sooo…demons exist? Like, in real life?" Her eyes flicked to Kallie then to Theo. "What if I didn't have you two? Can you imagine how many other people are possessed like that?" She couldn't begin to imagine, she had so many questions, but more importantly she had so much anger inside of her, she wished so hard there was a way she could combat the supernatural, then she would make sure that demon and all of its kind would pay for this.

"Did Morgana kill it? The demon?" Hana asked sternly.

Theo's turn to answer. "Yes, there are demons, and most Mundanes never live through it long enough to tell or hear their tales on demonic possession. She didn't kill the demon, Hana, it is more complicated than that, but what is most important is that this will never happen again.”

“How sure are you about that? What if there is yet another demon angry at William enough to find and possess me?” She questioned eyes fiery.

“That won’t happen; Morgana cast a protection spell on you to keep you safe. No demon can possess or harm you—she made sure of that, I made sure she did.” Theo promised.

“That’s reassuring. So with this protection, can I fight demons? Because I sure as hell want to hunt some down!” Hana smirked.

“Now that’s the fire I missed.” Kallie teased, poking Hana lightly on the shoulder. “I am serious though, can I?” Hana turned her gaze to Theo, and he knew then how serious she was.

“Only with proper training Hana, demon hunting is really dangerous.”

“You know how I can get that training?”

“If you are truly serious, I have some contacts.” Theo answered. “But for now, I need both your help for All Hallows Eve.”

Kallie’s eyes met his as his jaw clenched, his mood turning serious once more.

CHAPTER EIGHTEEN

It was the thirty first day of October and that meant one thing for the rest of the world and another for Theo, Kallie, and Hana.

They drove through the east end of Amherst, passing homes covered in decorations ready for Trick or Treaters; their headlights bouncing off carved pumpkins and decorated porches. As they approached the last few neighborhoods before the forests started; the crowds and decorations became less and less before there was nothing but trees lining the road. Kallie stared out the window from the front seat of her beloved car, Theo in charge of driving this time. He squeezed her hand lightly sensing her nerves. Kallie had always loved Halloween, even as a kid when her Dad would take her Trick or Treating, she loved the whimsy of it all, the decorations and apple cider. She loved watching the kids and teenagers enjoy their Halloween night, going around neighborhoods for candy. Her thoughts briefly found their way to her Dad. *Had he known about Mom? Did he know about me, what I really was?* Answers she would never receive.

They arrived at an abandoned church building. Morgana's guide had led them to it, located in the middle of a huge deserted field. It looked more like the ruins from some kind of natural disaster, as they walked closer to the church they noticed the doors were ancient and covered with cobwebs. Surely no one had been here in centuries. Morgana had mentioned the sacrifice was to be carried out by seven selected witches, each one holding down her side of a heptagon representing the entrances and exits of souls from all seven realms. Although Kallie thought this was the creepiest thing she had ever heard of, she knew she had to stop being the negative about this, especially because of how much Theo needed this.

"Since no one else is wondering, I will ask, why are witches using an old deserted church for a coven?" Kallie asked, feeling so weird in this place—the air brushing up against her skin felt different, too chill and depressing.

"Because this church is sacred ground, it was created this way to look like a church although it has never truly been one." Theo replied, as they walked inside, stepping over broken branches and twisting vines.

"Then why do they call it a church if it never was one?" Hana asked. Kallie was glad she did, she had the same question lingering in her mind.

"Because it was created to play host to the gathering of the supernatural. This is where all witches, demons, angels, and the rest of the underworld find common ground." William's voice answered huskily. He had not said a word the entire trip until now, and she could only imagine how he must be feeling, giving up his life and soul so willingly, and walking freely to his own death. Kallie's stomach felt heavy at the thought. Although he had done some awful things she still wasn't entirely okay with sacrificing someone.

They stood in a line just inside the door; Theo looked at his watch again. "It's eleven o'clock, I think we're just in time." He said, but none of them dared to move first. The tension was tangible between all of them. Theo turned to his Uncle William, and said, "I know it doesn't seem like it, but I am grateful for this, for offering to do this with me, for me." William's eyes were heavy; "I needed to do this, not just for you, but for me, for my own peace."

Theo turned to Kallie grabbing her by the waist, "I love you." And covered her lips with his, his mouth urgent, aware this may be their last, "I love you too." she spoke back, her throat becoming tight with emotion.

They walked into the hallway, each one following the other closely. The church had a powerful stench. The smell of death was so strong it made the short hairs at the back of Kallie's neck stand. They found the witches in no time, each one wearing a black garment covering their entire bodies, with a cloak covering their faces. They each held a wooden staff; each one standing already at all sides of the large heptagon holding their staffs out in front of them. Kallie looked around, nothing about this place deemed it fit to be called a church for whatever reason. She looked at the witches again, trying to spot Morgana even though she knew she couldn't—they were all the same, all shrouded.

It was eleven forty and just as the huge ancient clock clicked high up on the wall above them, Theo and William walked into the heptagon before kneeling in the center, their arms gripping each other's forearms tightly. As Morgana had instructed, all they had to do was hold onto each other and synchronize their breathing, binding themselves into one as much as they could.

For souls to be swapped they must first become one.

The witches hummed from within themselves almost immediately, each one chanting different spells at intervals, and Hana stood watching from the side, hands held tight together in good will. At eleven fifty, ten minutes to the swap hour, there was a rumble high up above them, a dark mist formed above their heads. Kallie and Hana grew tense and even more disturbed— Morgana had mentioned a rift opening during this exercise but she had not mentioned this dark mist covering them entirely, Kallie had a bad feeling, and she wasn't alone.

"I have come for what is mine!" A familiar voice rose from the shadow, a voice Kallie could never forget in a hurry. She ran towards the heptagon and Hana followed immediately after, but they were both thrown off by an invisible force coming from the witches' connection.

The witches started chanting even louder, their voices thundering, as they each raised the wooden staffs they held high above their heads in a bid to fight off the demon.

"I told you I would be back, and I've got company." The demon laughed loudly, the sound of his voice echoing severely in the ears of all who heard.

The witches focused on their chants. The thoughts of what could go wrong flooded Kallie's mind. Her eyes dashed wildly to Theo who was still locked arm in arm with William. She tried to access the heptagon again, and this time she felt the need to pull out her necklace from under her shirt, the stone in the pendant came to life, she could feel it throbbing in her hands like a pulse every second, and it charged even more with each passing thud. The light grew stronger and she managed to force her entrance into the heptagon. The demons above them scattered all over the room, each fighting with an opponent.

"We need to focus on the ritual—this is our only chance, it's less than two minutes, we can hold up." It was Morgana. Kallie stared at the clock and knew she was right. She tried to control and directing the light from her necklace at the dark mists, causing them to growl and scream in pain, while Morgana and the other witches focused on the ritual, they resumed their chants, *only two minutes more* she thought to herself. Chaos ensued around her; witches were being thrown from the circle by demons even as they tried to fend them away. The wind whirled loudly inside the church, leaves and debris flew through the air and Kallie's hair whipped at her face. She yelled for Theo, his face a blur through the smoke. Demonic smoke engulfed Kallie tugging against her clothes, her necklace ripped from her neck and thrown across the room while demons cackled.

Something hit Hana hard and sharp, cutting her thigh deeply. She cried out causing Kallie to turn and rush towards Hana, but she didn't reach her before she felt the darkness smash her skin, heavy like a wave of water pushing her down, drowning her. She didn't see what hit her, but it was dark, deep, and drifting. She felt her body give way, and then there was nothing else. Just darkness.

* * *

The smoke cleared the clock striking 12:01am. William lay in the middle of the circle broken, his soul gone never to return. "Kallie, please wake up!" Hana cried minutes later. They watched Theo cry in agony and pain as he held onto Kallie's unconscious body, his body shaking violently. He said no words, just wailed, growled, and screamed at intervals, as if the sound of his voice was the only thing that could bring her back.

He could feel their gazes on him. This was all his fault, he couldn't stop the images of her sweet smiling face filled with worry as she begged him time and time again to let go of this ritual, she had always felt that something would go wrong, and she was right. It did go wrong, everything went wrong. William's soul was taken to purgatory by the army of demons at the eleventh second, and the very woman he wanted to spend all of his mortal days with lay lifeless in his arms.

Morgana noticed the dim lighting from Kallie's necklace fade lightly. There was still light in it, she realized there was still life in Kallie. What she was not sure of was for how long she could hold on.

"What can we do?" Hana looked frantically at Morgana. "There has to be something, please!"

"Nothing can be done, not from here, and she cannot make it long enough to get out."

"There has to be something?!" Hana yelled at Morgana frustrated.

"What if I turn her?" Theo's solemn face rose to eye them both halting their arguing.

"She isn't exactly mundane remember, and we both know fairy and night children don't mix, you just may create a monster, or it kills her. She may never wake up again." Morgana flitted her hands sadly, flashing her long, black nails.

Theo's mind raced, he knew he didn't have the time to start weighing options, whatever it was, he was prepared to face it—if this was Kallie's only chance at survival, he wouldn't forgive himself for not letting her have it. He looked at Hana; her tear streaked face met his and she nodded in agreement kneeling beside them.

He bit down onto his wrist, the blood hitting the stone floor before he lifted it to Kallie's open lips. The blood trailed into her mouth some dripping down her chin. He kissed her forehead his hands grasping her face tightly, "I'm so sorry…" Kallie's breathing stopped, her heart faltering.

Ba boom… Ba boom… Ba…

CHAPTER NINETEEN

Kallie awoke to the smell of the wind, the all too familiar scent of Amherst. It did not brush up her skin like it should but she smelled the wind, the green life pushing through the trees, plants and flowers, she could hear the sounds of birds chirping and wondered how deep into the forest she had to be to feel it so close. She opened her eyes to find herself staring at the white vintage ceiling in Theo's bedroom, the white sheets of his bed curled around her softly. She turned her head to find Theo staring at her closely, she smiled and immediately they locked eyes. Theo smiled back at her. "Kallie…" He pulled her close, he smelled so strong like he was wearing double the cologne. She caressed his chest as he kissed her deeply, he tasted different too.

"Hi" she chirped. "What's going on?"

Hana burst through the door, "Kallie, oh my God! You had us so fucking worried, it has been five days. Five. Whole. Days!" Hana breathed the words against Kallie's skin as she reached out to hug her tightly, she squeezed Kallie so hard she was scared she would break her in that one hug. Kallie could hear the blood running through Hana's veins as she held on to her, she felt the irresistible desire to place her lips on Hana's skin and just keep sucking on it until she could taste the blood rush into her mouth, she suddenly felt hungry just thinking of how satisfying that would feel.

She felt different, odd— evil for thinking of how much she would relish the taste of her own best friend's blood.

She withdrew from the hug and pushed Hana away lightly. She had so many questions like: why was she thinking about how good blood tastes, *why was she so hungry at the thought of it, why could she hear, smell and feel everything from miles away?*

"Five… days?" Kallie repeated confused, rubbing her temple. "What happened?"

She looked to Theo for answers, surely there was an explanation to all this she thought, and if anyone had the answers to the questions in her head then it was Theo, but first she needed to know how the ritual had gone. As much as she tried, she remembered nothing after hearing Hana scream for help. She remembered Hana again, and turned to look at her. *She looked okay* she thought, but that was the last thing about the ritual she could remember. "Is anyone going to tell me how the ritual went? And why I don't remember anything else from last night? …Five nights ago." She corrected herself quickly.

"William didn't make it. The demons they…they took his soul to purgatory." Theo explained. Kallie stared at him wide eyed, "No…does that mean?" "Yes, I'm still a vampire." Theo said sighing, finishing her sentence.

"We nearly lost you too, Kallie." Hana continued, "Theo saved you." Kallie glanced back at Theo, his eyes were cast downwards. "I'm so sorry…" he said "I had no other choice, I… I had to turn you."

Kallie stared at Theo wide eyed, then back at Hana. "Wait…does that make me a vampire?"

Theo nodded his head slightly, and said, "We weren't sure if it would even work, vampire and Fae are not normally mixed." Theo replied lightly.

"And did it work?" She stood abruptly to look in the big mirror next to the bed, Hana and Theo eyeing her cautiously. Although she felt different, really different, she did not look so different physically she thought—she looked hard again and her eyes widened. She blinked then looked hard again, her left pupil was her usual bright green but her right pupil was a burning shade of amber. The same colour as Theo's. Her hands touched her mouth lightly in shock. She reached for her necklace and felt the pendant thud again in reaction to her touch. "My eyes," she turned back to them both shocked.

"I know," Theo replied. "You seem to be half vampire, half fae."

"They're pretty amazing, Kallie." Hana exclaimed beaming.

She turned back towards the mirror. *Does she have fangs?* She opened her mouth to examine her teeth, but she did not find what she expected, her fangs were much smaller than Theo's, only slightly longer than her normal teeth but still sharp. She touched one and winced as it let out a small droplet of blood. Kallie smiled, her fangs shining in the sunlight. Theo wrapped his arms around her from behind hugging her tightly, holding her close enough so that she could feel him deep under her skin, and whispered softly, almost inaudibly, "You mean the world to me, I don't want this world without you in it. I am so sorry I had to do this without giving you the chance to choose for yourself."

"You did what was right Theo—you saved my life, and I love you even more for this gift, to spend forever by your side. To be with you for eternity."

Hana jumped in laughing creating a group hug as they relished the lives they only just survived with that Halloween night. And in that moment Kallie felt grateful for all they had been through together and the amazing gift that Theo had given her.

She would cherish it forever. *Literally.*

EPILOGUE

Kallie looked through the back window of Theo's apartment, sitting cross legged her thoughts drifting to the outside world. She never realised how much she'd missed the small things before. The smiles of parents and happy children walking through the park, cars driving by, and birds in the trees. She hadn't been out in months; although a month for a vampire felt like a day. Kallie had to control her blood lust first or risk a massacre. But she really needed to get back to work. Hana had been of immense help dropping off messages at the university and picking up her work files, at first her boss had suggested that she stopped working altogether since she was seemingly too ill to make it to the university. Hana had been instrumental in finding a junior lecturer to cover for her, while the leftover work was taken home to Kallie.

She let her mind wander to Hana; she smiled at the thought of how much her best friend had grown in the past few months. She had been so determined to hunt demons after their Halloween experience that Theo had taken her to the Blade Sisters to practice how to kick ass; a cult of women sworn into bounty hunting and demon fighting. Although Hana's training with them isn't over until next Halloween, she had shown such confidence and dedication that she was permitted to go demon hunting on her own already.

Kallie had never seen Hana happier or more satisfied as she was about her new life as a bounty hunter. She replayed images of Hana chatting excitedly about her new life and all of her endless adventures as a bounty hunter. *It was amazing how much difference a few months could have on a person,* Kallie thought. It's crazy how easily it can all change. Just one night.

Breaking from her train of thought, she sensed another's presence as she turned around swiftly, her gaze catching his, his eyes pulling hers with a force almost physical even with just a stare. He looked as good as the first time she set eyes on him, and although she had changed these past few months, his effect on her body was stronger than ever—his magnetic pull affected not just her body but her mind. He intuitively knew when the other needed someone, like their minds were connected somehow. She was a part of him and he was a part of her in ways she was yet to understand, but she didn't mind. Nothing mattered but the touch and undying love of the one man her body and soul hungered for.

"I was looking for my Queen." He said, his voice cutting sharp and putting a stop to all of her thoughts. He walked closer to her; with each step she felt her own legs tremble. He rubbed his hands over her bare back, tracing his finger along the lines of her red satin dress, the dress he had asked her to wear tonight.

She wanted to ask about his queen, the one he was in search of, the one that was her. She wanted to say something smart and witty, but although she felt stronger than she had been all her life, although she could literally feel the energy surge through her own body, her lips trembled. He always had that effect on her. Even in immortality, he was her drug.

"Let's go."

www.ingramcontent.com/pod-product-compliance
Lightning Source LLC
Chambersburg PA
CBHW061539120726

48001CB00004B/1628